Three Red Hairs

Joanne McGough

Cover illustration Jan McLaughlin

Produced by Gingerbread Books

First edition June 2021 paperback

Joanne McGough

Three Red Hairs

ISBN: 9798501572287

For everyone who loves to read romance/mystery genre.

Three

Red

Hairs

Three Red Hairs

Surrey, England
Late March, 1967

Chapter 1

On this particularly rainy, late afternoon, a small, squarish black auto moved along a narrow country road at reasonable speed. There were no posted limits on a "B" road such as this one, for the rutted, rock-strewn lane imposed its own restrictions. Nevertheless, the auto was going fast enough to show that the driver most certainly had a destination to reach.

The driver, Miss Joanna Whitfield, was taking little notice of the lush English countryside as she drove her Morris Minor along this road, putting London and the M25 far behind her. Joanna's thoughts on this journey were not of the scenery but on the recent death of her father. He had been her hero and her only family since her mother's death, many years ago. She wondered what her future held. She'd no relatives left on her father's side. He'd been an only child whose parents died when Joanna was a young child.

While her father was ill, her chums and friends had given her full measure of support. But at his death Joanna inherited a tidy sum of money. In her friends' eyes she was no longer one-of-them.

Joanna and her friends Ellen and Nicholas taught at a private music conservatory in London. She and Ellen taught voice. Nicholas taught piano and accompanied the singers. Her work was frustrating at times. Rarely did she find a young child whose voice seemed promising. However, the parents of most of her pupils expected the voice teacher to work a miracle and change a voice that was mediocre at best into a finely tuned instrument.

Nicholas and Jo -- her nickname -- were engaged to be married, but that wedding would never take place. He had no money of his own and was too proud to marry hers. He and Ellen were now embarrassed in Jo's company. They urged her to strike out on her own, to audition for roles. She didn't need the meager income that teaching provided.

Ellen, who had always claimed that Joanna's voice was lovelier than her own, was effusive in her delight at Jo's inheritance and urged her to make a name for herself in the theatre. Privately, Joanna worried that at the age of thirty she was a bit "past it" to become a star. But Ellen urged her, just the same. Good former friend Ellen knew about this sweet little cottage near Maiden's Heath, Surrey, that was for sale. "It was my great-uncle's," Ellen said. "He was a recluse or a religious hermit or brother. He became funny in his head. But Rose Cottage is lovely."

The Morris coursed along through the overhanging boughs of trees whose leaves had recently opened from buds. The leaves were a pale, early green and still dripping wet from rain that had temporarily ceased to deluge the countryside. An occasional drop still spattered onto the windscreen. However, Joanna could see dark clouds on the horizon and feared she would have a formidable storm to drive through before arriving home.

As she drew nearer to those clouds, a steady rainfall began anew. Ahead she saw two women walking along the road. One figure, older than the other, body bent into the rain, carried an umbrella like a shield before her. She led the other figure by the hand, a young woman with black hair and skin the color of a bisque figurine. This young woman's hair was soaked into long strings but she didn't seem to care. She was waving her free arm back and forth in time to some melody only she could hear.

Joanna pulled the Morris up alongside the two women. Reaching back, she rolled down the passenger window and called out to them, "May I give you a lift, ladies?"

At first the older woman protested, "Oh we're wet already, miss. Don't trouble yourself."

But Joanna had only to insist a bit and the older woman accepted her offer. She bent down and entered through the auto's rear door, pulling the younger woman in beside her, addressing her as Lily while urging her to hurry. They settled themselves in the back seat and said nothing as Jo put the car in gear and drove on

Soon Joanna sensed that Lily was shifting about in the backseat. Jo looked into the rear-view mirror and was surprised to see Lily staring back at her. Jo quickly averted her eyes and studied the road ahead but she could feel Lily's stare persisting. When the girl reached out and touched Jo's hair, the older woman pulled her arm back and admonished Lily to have a care.

After a moment of silence, Joanna offered, "I'm headed for the village of Maiden's Heath. Can I drop you off near there?"

"The High Street will be just fine," the older woman said.

In the rear-view mirror Jo again made eye contact with the strangely smiling Lily and saw the girl again reach out to touch her hair. Quickly, the other passenger pulled Lily's arm back. Jo noticed the expression on the girl's face, her far away, enigmatic smile, never changed. The older woman however, appeared to be tense and worried. She held onto the girl's two hands but managed to say, "I think she likes your red hair, miss."

Joanna replied, "Don't worry yourself. We'll get to the High Street in just a few minutes. You would have had a good two miles to walk!" She was madly curious about her two passengers. *Were they mother and daughter? No, she thought, they're too far apart in years for that. But there is a definite resemblance.*

Lily might be about twenty years old. A lovely girl, really. Her hair was dark and hung in wet ringlets. The other woman looked like a time-worn, faded version of Lily, her hair was streaked with gray, her skin sallow.

Joanna thought she might be about sixty years old; however, she seemed strong. Joanna also suspected that in younger years this aging woman was no doubt a beauty.

The Morris slowed as it entered the village. Joanna turned the auto onto the High Street and pulled up to the curb. No sooner had she come to a stop than the nameless woman opened the car door and exited, pulling Lily along with her.

"Do you live near here?" Joanna asked as Lily was leaving the auto.

"She won't answer ya," the older woman said gruffly. "She never speaks."

Hoping for a friendlier response, Jo called out, "My name is Joanna Whitfield. I'm new in the village."

"I know who y'are, miss," the woman replied. She walked away, keeping Lily close by.

Joanna sat in her auto for a while, trying to digest her encounter with the two unusual women. She lowered the window and let some of the cool rain splash her face, hoping this would clear her thoughts. She was disappointed by her new acquaintances; there seemed to be no friendliness on their part. She would have to ask her neighbor, Hettie McEldoo about them.

<h1 align="center">Chapter 2</h1>

Joanna had moved to Maiden's Heath almost a month ago. She loved her little home with its oak wood floors, its old-fashioned "Cabbage Rose" wallpaper. The stone fireplace was a special treat.

"Rose Cottage," as the previous owner named it, immediately felt like home to her. Many days she walked throughout the house slowly, lingering in each room, tenderly touching the walls and furniture, or just standing in the middle of each room and sensing the calmness there. It all felt safe, welcoming.

Joanna recognized this ability to sense energy when she was but a young girl. Her mother taught her to trust those feelings and instincts. But they hadn't been as strong in the past.

In Rose Cottage the protective feeling was stronger than ever before. It comforted her.

The village of Maiden's Heath, just two miles east of Rose Cottage, was a welcoming place with many small shops and businesses. The actual heath lay just beyond Joanna's property.

One had to pick their way through a portion of forest, one hundred feet of thick brush and trees, to enter the heath itself. The heath had been cleared many years ago by some strong, determined people. It became a field used for many purposes. Joanna chuckled when she thought of the reason for the village's name.

Local lore had it that a couple of centuries ago, before a young maiden could marry, she had to walk a straight line across the heath wearing a mask covering her eyes. Her fiancé's mother made the blindfold. If the mother approved of the girl, she would cover her eyes with the sheerest gauze. Thus, the girl could "walk the line" accurately and marry her love. If the future mother-in-law didn't like the girl, she covered the girl's eyes with an opaque cotton cloth. The poor maiden would flail about and wander off course. Her fiancé would denounce her and marry someone else.

Joanna thought the village lovely but reserved. The shops were small and owned and managed by congenial local folk

Except for Hettie McEldoo and her husband, though, no one had actually tried to befriend her. However, everyone she met had been polite. Surely most of the villagers knew of her recent move there. It shouldn't surprise her then that this sole woman knew who she was.

Joanna became aware that the two women were standing under the awning of the green grocer's shop. But the rain became lighter and the older woman ventured out, checking how wet the air might be.

Jo did not intend to offer the two women another ride. She wanted to get home and ask Mrs. McEldoo

about them. She shut the auto's window, put her right
foot on the gas pedal, let out the clutch and the Morris
sped ahead, down the High Street.

Chapter 3

As she drove away, Joanna gave little thought to the women she'd dropped off. The rain continued to fall but was much lighter in volume. Still, her auto's headlamps didn't provide much visibility on the dark road. The two-mile drive to her cottage seemed to take far too long, but eventually she pulled into her own mud drive.

The light was on in her parlor window and from the smoke rising above the chimney, she knew that her neighbor, Mrs. McEldoo, had been over to tend to things.

Jo leaped from her auto and sprinted to the cottage, dodging raindrops as best she could. She found the cottage door unlocked and indeed, Mrs. McEldoo still there.

"Oh, you've finally got home, have you?" The smiling country woman greeted her. Not for the first time, Joanna thought that if her own mother had lived she would be warm and nurturing like this woman.

"Let me take those wet things," Hettie said as she helped Joanna slip out of her coat and shoes.

"I'm surprised to see you here so late," the tired and grateful redhead replied.

"Oh, I was home a while ago but when the hour got late and you weren't here yet, I came back to stoke the fire and put some heat under the soup."

At hearing these kind words, Jo wrapped her arms around the woman's plump figure and declared, "You are a love. What would I do without you!"

The good lady returned the hug. "Now," she insisted as she sat Jo by the fire, "you wait here and warm yourself. I'll bring your soup and tea."

Joanna could hear her friend in the kitchen. She found the noises coming from there -- the chinking of china, the kettle whistling -- very homey and comfortable. She sat quietly by the fire, enjoying the blessing of its warmth. Her mind wandered.

She called into the kitchen. "Mrs. McEldoo. This morning, before I left for London, I was looking out my bedroom window and I think I saw a large house up on the hillside. Who lives there?"

Hettie came into the parlor carrying a tray laden with steaming food. As she sat the tray down on a table near Joanna, she sighed with relief. "So, you can see his house. Not everyone can. The house belongs to Mr. Tony Lewis."

"The conductor? The composer? No."

"Yes!" Hettie laughed.

"Well I can't believe it. Does he come into the village?" Jo was excited and her voice betrayed it.

"Mr. Lewis likes his privacy, he does. We don't see much of him," Hettie offered. "Sometimes he comes into the village for market day. He's polite but he doesn't stop to chat. Usually his housekeeper does the shopping."

Joanna considered this for a moment, then declared, "I must meet him. I will meet him."

Mrs. McEldoo only smiled. She donned her coat and retrieved her umbrella from the closet. But another thought prompted Joanna to ask her friend to stay. "Mrs. McEldoo, wait please," she implored.

"Call me Hettie, darling, and of course I'll wait." She sat her becoated body down in a great, cozy chair and made herself comfortable.

Chapter 4

"**M**rs. Mac - - Hettie. I wonder if you can identify two women for me? I was about two miles east of Maiden's Heath, driving through the rain, and I saw two women walking on the road. They were quite wet and I offered them a lift. At first, they said no, or rather the older one did. The younger one never said a word. They weren't a bit friendly and the younger one was a bit queer in the head, I think. Anyway, they did get in the Morris. I dropped them off on the High Street."

Mrs. McEldoo had already deduced the identity of those two women. "A strange you girl with no words and an older woman? The girl was black haired? Very fair?"

Joanna nodded in agreement. "The older woman called her Lily."

"Yes, indeed," Hettie murmured, more to herself than aloud. She took off her coat while still seated, then settled back. She sighed, folding her arms across her ample bosom.

"You know them?" Joanna speculated.

"I know of them and they know of me." She paused, collecting her thoughts. Then she explained, "The older woman is Moraig Dunne. Lily is her grand daughter. Lily's mother was Trilby Dunne."

"Moraig's daughter Trilby was a black-haired beauty, too. She died when Lily was but a few months old."

"Moraig Dunne is no one to play with," Hettie continued. "She does some private nursing for folks and she takes Lily with her on every job. They say she never lets the girl out of her sight."

Hettie was quiet for a short while. She was pondering the subject, deciding how much to tell Joanna. She decided not to hold anything back, and began. "Some say that Moraig has a magic willow tree behind her cottage. She uses sticks from that tree to help girls get rid of babies they never meant to conceive. Babies still in the womb, if you get my meaning."

"She performs abortions with sticks form a tree!" Joanna shuddered. "How awful!"

"That it is, darling'," Hettie confirmed. "Some say she makes a potion that a girl can drink, It's for the same purpose. If the potion doesn't work, the girl pays more money and Moraig uses the willow stick."

"Why can't she be stopped?" Jo demanded.

"Because, darlin', there's a demand for her services. Keep mindful of the area we live in. These are farm girls, unsophisticated, poorly educated. Even the girls from the villages are too shy to go to a hospital."

"She sounds like an evil witch," Jo declared, as she slipped into the kitchen and quickly returned with a cuppa' for Hettie.

"Be careful how you use those words," Hettie admonished."

"Are there witches here?" Joanna was stunned; her blue eyes grew round with alarm.

Hettie adjusted herself in the overstuffed chair before she answered. Then, "There are, but just a few. Pay them no mind. Years ago, there were many witches in the coven. They caused no harm. They just worshipped different from most people. They even had remedies for things that the doctor couldn't cure."

"But the Holy Brothers of the monastery at St. Edmund's didn't approve. The previous owner of your cottage was one. They came and purified the heath where the witches used to worship. The Brothers did their sanctifying with fire and holy water on the sunrise of All Hallows Eve. The coven had no place to worship and that was one of their high, holy times."

"Many of the witches left, but not before they warned the Brothers that they'd be back, even stronger than before. I haven't heard anything of them since."

Another pause brought a heavy silence in the room.

"You don't have to give one thought to the whole story," Hettie said. "Just stay clear of Moraig and Lily. Don't cross their path, don't offer them a ride. Don't ever need Moraig's services. You'll be alright."

Hettie extricated herself for the big, soft chair and donned her coat again. "I'll be going home now, my dear." She smiled fondly at the young woman. "Just stay clear of them."

Chapter 5

Joanna sat in silence after Hettie McEldoo left. Her thoughts were whirling. She was stunned by what Hettie told her and she needed to make sense of it all. She wasn't frightened, but she was certain that Moraig Dunne knew her identity. She decided that she would take Hettie McEldoo's advice to avoid the woman.

At eight pm she made her way up the stairs to her bedroom. She rarely went to bed this early, but she was weary. The trip to London had been tiring, nearly two hours' drive each way. The business which had taken her there was unpleasant: she had to collect her belongings for the music conservatory. She had a headache all the while she was dealing with former colleagues.

As she was packing the last of her music she chatted with some old friends. She found their questions predictable and exhausting: "How are you? How've you been? How do you like country living?" And of course, there were perfunctory statements: "We miss you. Good to see you again. Drop in any time you're in London."

Joanna pasted a smile on her face the minute she walked through the conservatory doors. The smile remained in place so long, her facial muscles hurt. The worst, most painful meeting was with Nicholas and Ellen. She'd told no one she was coming, so they were surprised to see her and uncomfortable in her presence.

The look of guilt on Nicholas' face was unmistakable. His smile was not spontaneous; it came only after he realized he should smile. He had to search for words to say to her.

"I'm surprised to see you." At least he'd been honest. "What are you doing here?" Rather blunt, Nicholas. "Actually, Ellen's here today. I, uh, know she'll want to see you. Stay right here. I'll run and get her."

"How pathetic he is," she thought. *"Thank God I'm not going to marry him. And being in bed with him was a waste of time. He was always in such a hurry."*

She hadn't long to wait for him to return. He must have known exactly where Ellen was for they both appeared in just a few minutes. Ellen was effusive in her delight to see Jo, but the gushing was phony. Anyone could tell. Ellen was en garde' against Joanna and was fairly glued to Nicholas' side. Joanna was sure they were lovers.

"How great to see you!" Ellen slobbered as she kissed the air beside Joanna's face. "Country life agrees with you," Ellen crooned. "You've put on a few pounds!"

"It is great to see both of you." Jo's smile was frozen on her face. It hurt a lot, but then, so did her spirit.

She was determined, however, not to let these two phonies see how much pain she was in. "I wish I could visit longer, but I must dash! If you're ever out in the country, drop in for a visit. Ellen, you surely know where I live! Ta, loves!" She blew them a kiss, turned smartly and walked away.

She got all the way to the Morris before tears overflowed her eyes. She silently cursed her two false friends. *"The only good thing Ellen ever did for me was to put me onto her uncle's cottage,"* she thought.

Driving out of London on the M25 had been a nerve-wracking experience, as usual. The rain began even before she exited onto the 'A' road. When she turned onto the 'B' road her progress slowed considerably. Her drive home through the rain and her encounter with the two curious women left her exhausted.

She fell asleep immediately.

Chapter 6

When Lily and her grandmother exited the Morris, they hurried across the street to a shelter provided by the green grocer's awning. Moraig Dunne was breathing heavily from the effort of moving the girl along and from her frustration with Lilly's actions in the auto.

"What did ya think ya were doin'girl!" Moraig admonished. "Ya were that brazen, touchin' ' er 'air like that twice then tryin' for a third. Ya let her feel it! Ya must be wily, artful. Ya must make yer touch light."

In reply, Lily smiled vacantly and looked puzzled. She could tell by the tone of Moraig's voice that her grandmother was angry, but the girl couldn't understand why. She'd done what Moraig taught her to do.

Moraig's attention was drawn to the fact that Joanna's auto hadn't moved. She pulled Lily back closer to the building where they stood in shadow. There they would wait until the rain eased up. Then they would move on.

After a few minutes the deluge did lessen and Joanna drove away. Moraig cautiously stepped out from the awning. .She held up the palm of one hand to the damp air. Satisfied that the rain was light now, Moraig took Lily by the hand and pulled her along the quiet street.

Soon they came to a narrow alley which Moraig entered without hesitation. The alley was dark and damp, but she seemed to know just where she was going. Lily had no choice but to follow.

The alley led them between high stone walls which had a decaying dank smell. "I wonder if this path ever sees the light of day," Moraig muttered, but she kept up her determined pace.

The alley brought them out onto a poorly lit, cobblestone street. Shops along the street had not prospered as the ones on the High Street had. Indeed, many of the store fronts had boarded-over windows and seemed to have been vacant for a long time. The boards were stained from the weather and now were buckled instead of being flat. The window frames were mostly rotted.

The two women turned left onto the street and passed the empty shops without paying them any heed. At the end of this street, they came to a mews.

Most of the mews was as dark as the street that led to it. There was, however, a single light on, shining above the dark, purple door of a tiny, semi-detached, stone house. The other half of the structure had been vacated years ago.

In the daylight an observer could've read the black letters on the purple door:

Maven Scarlett

Herbalist

Nurse

In the darkness of this damp night, though, the letters weren't visible. Only the light above the door identified the site. It was to this light and door that Moraig and Lily were going. And perhaps they had been there before, as a faint glimmer of recognition appeared on Lily's face.

When the women reached the door, Moraig didn't step into the light. Instead, she stood a little to one side, keeping Lily close behind her. She rapped three times on the door. It was opened promptly from inside. The girl and the woman hurried in.

They stepped into a darkened hallway and were met by a woman holding a single candle. She led them to a room at the end of the passage. They entered the room silently. Their hostess closed the door quietly behind them, then reached up with her free hand and clicked on a wall lamp.

The lamp was not of a generous wattage; it provided just enough illumination to make navigation within the room possible.

The room itself was small, rectangular and not overly furnished. There was only one window, that being on the wall opposite the door through which the women had entered. The window was completely obscured by a heavy drape of a velvety texture. The drape served the purpose of preventing daylight from intruding through the window and indeed, had served this purpose for a very long time. The fabric was so encrusted by dirt that its color could not be determined. Webs of dust grew from the drape to the wall beside it.

In the middle of the room was a round, oak table. This was in such disproportion to the dimensions of the room, there was just enough space to walk around it.

Their hostess extinguished her candle then turned up the flame in a corner gas heater. She took her place at the table, facing her two guests.

Chapter 7

The woman who escorted Moraig and Lily into this suspicious little chamber was the proprietress of the establishment, Maven Scarlett. It was she who spoke first.

"Greetings to you, Sister Moraig, and to you, my sweet Sister Lily." She smiled warmly at the young girl. Lily smiled in return, her fascination with Maven Scarlett showed on her glowing face.

Mother Maven was an extraordinary looking woman. Her complexion was uncommonly fair, her hair hung long below her shoulders and was a soft, silver color. She had eyes that were of the palest blue but capable of intense focus.

At times she seemed to be quite small. However, when needed, she could appear to be much larger. She moved with the grace of a ballerina, her feet barely touching the ground. But she was far from being delicate. Her smallest, most gentle gesture could reveal a power and authority uncommon in both ordinary women and witches.

To Lily, Mother Maven was enchanting. To Moraig she was a powerful presence to be served. She returned Maven's salutations. "Greetin' and honor ta you, Mother Maven, daughter of the goddess," she said respectfully. "We come as soon as we got yer message."

Maven smiled benevolently. She spread her arms open, extending one hand to Moraig and the other to Lily. They formed a small circle though only the fingertips touched. They all bowed their heads and Maven Scarlett hummed softy, once, then again, then again. Slowly she pushed back her chair and rose to her feet. She lifted her arms into the air. The other two women followed her example.

With their arms raised high and eyes closed they began to sway gently, rhythmically, humming a high-pitched note. A soft 'pat, pat-pat, pat' sounded upon the table. As the women opened their eyes, they saw the source of the sound. A small, delicate cat with a coat of shimmering silver stood on the middle of the table.

The cat arched its back and extended its tail. Slowly and sensually it stretched its neck, its legs and its hips as though trying to work out the kind of stiffness one gets after too long a sleep. Once limbered, the animal looked directly toward Maven Scarlett, mewed in recognition and leaped gently into her arms.

Mother Maven welcomed the cat. She stroked it, nuzzling her face into its nearly luminous fur. She whispered, "Hello, Goddess *Aoefe." Moraig Dunne was relieved to see the cat. She sighed deeply and smiled like a person who knows she is in the company of a being greater than herself.

Lily purred like a wee kitten in a voice more befitting a three-year-old child. She reached out her arms toward Maven and the cat, and whimpered wordlessly her desire to hold the animal. But Maven was not willing to share her familiar. "Not yet," she said kindly. "Not until your hair is as silver as mine. Then, perhaps Goddess Aoefe may be yours."

Moraig took hold of Lily's entreating arms and pulled them back away from the cat. "I'm sorry Mother Maven," she said. "Ya know how Lily is. There's no telling' wh' goes on in 'er 'ead."

"Sister Moraig, don't fret about Lily. We all know. Her mother could have been the most powerful of us all. Goddess Aoefe has told me that Lily will be changed one day. We must wait."

She continued, "Goddess Aoefe has also told me there is another, a mystic woman, nearby. Not one of us. I have sensed her presence recently."

"Another witch!" Moraig was stunned.

"No, perhaps not a witch. But she is a strong, spiritual woman. And powerful, in her way. Her energy is quite young. She may not know the extent of her power yet."

Then refocusing on Lily, Maven declared, "What an awesome task you've been given, Sister Moraig. What an honor, to raise and guide Lily, to keep her safe." She rose from her chair and asked, "Will you please excuse me for a moment? Some of our other sisters are arriving."

As Mother maven left the room, she closed the door behind her. As soon as Moraig was sure she couldn't be heard, she demanded of Lily, "Let me have those hairs from that girl's head."

Lily blushed in response. She knew she completed a task and her grandmother should be pleased. She reached into the pocket of her dress and produced her trophy: three red hairs.

"Good girl," Moraig said appreciatively. She took the hairs from Lily's hand and placed them in a small, silk pouch. Hiding the pouch deep in her pocket, she murmured, "I may never have cause to use 'em. Or I might."

The door to the room opened and Mother Maven entered, along with three other women, each one older by far than Moraig Dunne.

"We are privileged, Moraig and Lily." Mother was obviously delighted. "These sisters were here years ago, when our sacred heath was decimated by the Christian brothers. The sisters have been away, but they've practiced our craft and remained strong. They'll help us to rebuild our coven."

1

---

*Aoefe -- pronounced E fa - a princess in Irish mythology.

Chapter 8

The women's meeting was brief and to the point. After introductions were given, Maven explained that their primary concern was to reclaim the heath. They should all meet at the heath just before sunrise two days from then, on Sunday morning with bunches of sage and cedar bark. They would burn these items and, using large feathers, spread the smoke over the heath as they smudged it, thus purifying the area and inviting kind spirits to join them.

Moraig would enjoy the process. She would use sage from her own garden. She would also hunt through the forest for cedar trees. She knew they would be scarce, but finding even one would yield plenty of bark.

As Moraig and Lily made their way home from the convening, Moraig was elated. She walked with a light step, occasionally swinging her umbrella back and forth. "We'll get it all back," she happily proclaimed. "Soon the heath will be ours." She laughed out loud.

In response to Moraig's festive mood, Lily tore loose from her grandmother's hand and ran out onto the High Street. She twirled and danced with delight.

To the untrained she would have appeared to be just a happy young woman. But Moraig recognized the pattern that Lily was dancing. Lily was celebrating too, by dancing deasil, making a circle like a clock, turning right.

"Nay child," Moraig said as she took Lily by the arm and pulled her along toward home. "Ya canna' do that dance in public. Folks will be suspicious."

They walked on, quickening their steps. They walked the two miles going east of the village until they came upon a rayless path which led directly into a dense wood. The path was nearly obscured by a proliferation of weeds, brambles, and saplings that had no chance to grow, given the overhead boughs and branches. The path was nearly a mile long and difficult to follow even in daytime when a modicum of dappled sunlight did what it could to show the way. The path led to Moraig's home.

On this foggy night the path could hardly be determined. No rational person would have attempted to traverse it. Moraig, however, knew the way very well. She'd lived in this small, wooden home since she was twenty years old, when she and her infant daughter, Trilby were given it by the coven.

The coven feared that her infant's energy and demands would interfere with their meditation and their silent times. Thus, Moraig and Trilby must not live in their communal home.

Her sister witches had cleansed the house and the land around it by smudging. They cut down saplings, small trees and bushes and created a clearing around the house where sunshine could penetrate. Moraig was expected to grow herbs and flowers that would be used for healing, for love and well-being. Moraig planted other herbs for purposes not as noble. Her sister witches weren't aware of these.

The coven members intended no harm to anyone; however, their own safety was sometimes in jeopardy. Townspeople generally let them live as they wished, but if a tragedy occurred, if there was a flu epidemic, if a child went missing, the winter too cold or the summer too hot, the witches were blamed.

First rumors would start, then threats would follow. No witch was physically harmed but she might be shunned by the townspeople or she might be denied service at a shop. The citizens of Maiden's Heath were unaware that members of the coven were working to reverse the unhappy situations.

Moraig's garden grew bountifully due to sunlight that was made available and the temperate climate. There was Angelica root to hang in the kitchen and summon protective angels. Beautiful pink and purple Heather had abundant presence and would bring good luck. Lavender in shades of silvery green and purple would attract a husband for a maiden lady. There was Sage, always necessary to drive out bad spirits, and Chives for the same purpose.

Moraig sold Basil to young women who were trying to conceive. They were to hang a bunch of it over the bed and make love under it every night for two weeks. A pouch of dill hung above the nursery door ensured that infants would have good intelligence. Mint brought angels. Rosemary would bless the home.

Scattered throughout the garden were white flowers that were unfamiliar to most people. The red variety of this flower was easily recognized as poppy. Moraig learned years ago the white poppy had the same nature and properties as the red. Furthermore, the white was a smaller plant more easily tucked away under other herbs.

She knew how to gather and wash poppy seeds and make seed tea. She knew that if the seeds weren't washed, the tea could be fatal, for the seeds contained Morphine, in amounts that couldn't be predicted. Also, the tea could cause hallucinations or become addictive.

She also knew how to extract opium from the poppy bulb. She didn't intend to do that unless no other tool in pharmacopeia would do the job.

Moraig's purported reason for growing poppies was to make a seed and milk paste that she sold to women as a skin moisturizer. Indeed, there were requests for this product every Wednesday, market day in Maiden's Heath. Moraig always attended, taking Lily with her. They both carried baskets full of dried herbs and flowers. Everything sold well.

The sister witches, even Maven Scarlett, knew nothing of Moraig's full arsenal of poppies. They were aware of only a few plants, those used to make the face cream.

They were also unaware of the presence of another powerful herb, Lobelia. In large doses Lobelia caused vomiting and diarrhea. The abdominal cramping was excruciatingly painful and could cause a pregnant woman to expel her fetus. This was Moraig's magic potion that pregnant girls sought. It usually worked quite well.

They reached the cottage easily and silently. Once inside Moraig lit a candle and an oil lamp. She instructed Lily to get ready for bed.

While Lily was busy in her preparations, Moraig cautiously removed the silk pouch from her pocket. She checked to see that the red hairs were still there, then placed the pouch between pages of her book of 'Olde Magik'. The pages she chose told the story of Isobel Gowdie, a famed, red-haired Scots witch from the 17th century. Moraig closed the book, satisfied that the hairs were safe.

Chapter 9

The next morning Joanna awakened easily but she was reluctant to pull herself out from the warmth of her down comforter and tried to burrow into her pillows. She thought she might have a lazy day.

Her reverie was abruptly halted by a loud knock on the cottage door. *What a bloody bother*, she thought. She climbed out of bed and, donning a robe and slippers, hurried to the door. She was met there by Mr. Horace McEldoo.

"Mornin' miss," he greeted and tipped his cap in the true country fashion. "The missus sent me over to help with the gardenin' ya was goin' ta do."

Joanna had completely forgotten about that. She intended to start clearing out some furiously overgrown patches today, as the weather was forecasted to be sunny and mild. She'd mentioned her plan to Hettie yesterday. Hettie said the weeds would be easy to pull after all the rain the day before.

"Forgive me, Mr. Mac," she asked of him, knowing she had permission to address him by his familiar name. "Come in and put the kettle on, why don't you, while I run upstairs and get dressed."

"Nay, miss," he refused, tipping his cap again. "Had my mornin' meal a couple 'a hours ago. Just tell me where ta start. Join me when yer able."

"As you wish," she smiled. "At the back of the house, I think I've uncovered a patio of some sort-- some large, flat stones. They're close to the house. I'd like to clear out that patch."

Tipping his cap a third time, Mr. McEldoo cordially agreed. "Right you are!" He set off toward the back of the house, occasionally picking his way past some bramble or thorn bush.

Joanna called after him, "There are tools in the old shed."

The cap was waved in reply.

Jo watched his spry gait as he left for this morning's chore. She noticed, not for the first time, what exact opposites Hettie and Horace McEldoo were. He was as thin as she chubby. He was a man of few words; she was a talkative woman. But they were friendly, warm folk. Joanna was quite fond of them both.

Minutes later Joanna emerged from the house dressed for the chilly, damp, late March morning. She was thankful she had heeded Hettie's advice and picked up old clothes for the church's jumble sale. She wore old denim jeans, knee high wellies and an Irish wool jumper that was much too large, but loose and easy to move in. Her long, wavy, copper-red hair was pulled up into a loose tassel on the top of her head. She carried a beaker of hot tea in each hand, one for herself and one for Mr. Mac.

She found her neighbor hunkered down, pulling years of mossy growth from a bed of fieldstone. "Do you think there's any hope for it?"

Handing Mr. Mac his tea, she suggested, "I'd like to know how large this old patio is. Why don't you take a shovel and sort of pound around here? See if you can find the ends of it. I'll take over the grunt work."

Morning became noon, then afternoon. The day's early chill was replaced by a clear sky, sunshine and a warmer temperature. Joanna's back, hands and knees were aching from the arduous task of freeing stones of tenacious, rooted moss.

Between the stones grew huge weeds, some jagged, others smooth, some thin and erect, others flat leafed and sticky. Some weeds had been persistent enough to actually crack stones or lift them out of the ground.

Mr. Mac estimated that the patio was quite large and had been built in two levels. The kitchen door opened on the higher level. In the middle of this tier were two steps which led down to the lower level. "It makes good sense," he said, "seeing as how the property slopes so much."

They soon discovered, however, that the lower level was not a patio. The stones seemed to form a path which divided, half going right, half going left. The separation of the paths widened to a large expanse, then began to return to each other.

Mr. Mac stopped exploring the stone pattern. He lay down his shovel, revived his cap and took a minute to scratch his head. "Well I completely forgot about this," he declared.

Joanna didn't know what he was referring to so she didn't respond to his statement. The gentleman continued on with his thoughts. "Yes sir, I completely forgot what used to be here." He walked slowly, kicking at the weeds with the toe of his boot. "Yup," he stated, "it's still here."

"What's still here?" Jo was puzzled.

His voice implied that it was obvious. "The circle!"

Their work was pleasantly interrupted by the arrival of Mrs. Hettie McEldoo. The stout lady came carrying a large picnic basket of food. They would have a late lunch.

Joanna was delighted by her friend's arrival. She jumped up to carry the basket and hugged the woman gratefully. "I'm so happy to see you!" Jo exclaimed.

"I thought you might be hungry about now," Hettie chuckled.

"And thirsty, Mrs. Mac," her husband added.

"I knew that, Mr. Mac," Hettie replied. She spread a faded, cotton tablecloth on a cleared portion of the upper patio level and set out food and libation. She handed her husband a bottle of Harp lager, saying, "just the one, Mr. Mac."

"Just the one," he agreed.

"And for you, my lass, a Coca-Cola," Hettie offered.

"Wonderful!" Joanna hugged her again.

The three people found some cleared stones to sit on. They made short work of Hettie's ham sandwiches, then drank tea, still warm from the thermos. They ate silently, enjoying the sunshine and the sweet spring air.

Impulsively, Joanna asked, "Mr. Mac, what is the circle? What is it for?"

The McEldoos exchanged furtive glances. Mr. McEldoo indicated that his wife should begin. "I'll tell you the whole truth as I know it," she said. She glanced at her husband and he nodded in agreement.

"When Horace and I moved here, about twelve years ago, Father Stephen was still here, living in Rose Cottage. And the circle was already there. It was beautiful with a flower border. Velvety soft grass filled the middle. Father Stephen didn't use it at all, but late at night, on occasion ---"

"When the moon was full," Horace interjected.

"Not every month," Hettie corrected him, "but on an occasional full moon, we heard women's voices singing from the circle. We peeked out our window a few times and we could see the women, dancing in a circle, by candlelight. Every time, there was a young woman, seated on a chair, like a throne, and the women -- witches -- danced around her. She was dressed in white, like a bride."

"Did they sacrifice her?" Joanna gasped; her eyes open wide with alarm.

"No darlin' I'm sure they didn't," Hettie assured

her.

Mr. Mac took over at this point. "The day the Christian Brothers burned the heath, they also burned the circle."

Hettie continued, "After that, Father Stephen was never the same. A couple years later grass was growing back. The good priest had a beautiful statue of the Virgin Mary delivered and had it placed in the middle of the circle."

Joanna asked, "What happened to it? Where is it?"

Hettie replied, "No one knows. It disappeared one night."

Horace interrupted, "Just woke up one mornin' and it was gone."

"When was that exactly?" Jo wanted to know.

Hettie replied that she couldn't say exactly what year that was but it was near All Souls Day. The Holy Brothers wanted the heath for a celebration that night. It could have been nine or ten years ago.

They finished their lunch quietly. A few minutes later Horace stood up and stretched his thin frame as far as his back would bend. "Mrs. Mac," he said, "it's time for my siesta." He tipped his cap to both women then set off for home.

"Men!" Hettie complained.

Joanna's facial expression became a broad grin. "Speaking of men," she teased, "tell me more about Tony Lewis."

"Oh no you don't," Hettie scolded, while laughing. "I only know him to say 'hello' to. But I'll tell you what."

"Oh yes?"

"Tomorrow is market day. Come with me. Sometimes Mr. Lewis is there."

Chapter 10

By four pm Hettie declared she had to leave. She had Mr. Mac's tea to prepare, then dinner to start. "Come over about seven o'clock and share our meal," she invited.

"Maybe I will," Joanna mused aloud. "I want to work a bit longer. Then I'll indulge myself with a long, hot bath. I'll be there at seven, all clean and neat."

Joanna watched the pump figure of Hettie McEldoo as the woman made her way through the overgrowth of flora on Rose Cottage property, then on to her own swath of green grass. Jo sat for a while, considering the McEldoo couple. They seemed to know many people in Maiden's Heath. They had no children and very little other family. Hettie had a sister in Australia, Horace had a brother in Canada. They seemed to be adopting Joanna, unofficially of course, as their own. This pleased her. She was still young enough to appreciate parents.

She turned her attention to the curious stone circle and the weeds that defiled it. She knelt and proceeded to pluck more, but her hands and knees had become painful from this time-consuming work. *Enough for one day*, she decided.

After storing the spades and shovels in the shed, she took off her wellies and placed them just outside the kitchen door. The bathtub and hot water beckoned.

In just a few minutes she was soaking in a tub of deliciously warm water with plenty of lavender scented bubbles. Mindful of the time, she'd placed a windup clock on top of the toilet tank, glancing at it now and then.

When the clock hands pointed to six p.m., she pulled the cork from the drain but sat still to listen to the gobbling sound the drain pipe made as water surged through it. What she heard immediately was gurgle, gurgle, gulp, gasp, then gurgle, gurgle, gulp, gasp again. The sequence of noises persisted until the tub was emptied. Sometimes she stuck her heel into the drain to see if she could change the pattern. When she freed her heel, it was quite red but the sequence of noises never changed.

Joanna loved hearing all that, which in her mind was what a monstrously big dog would sound like lapping up water from a bucket and burping out air. It always amused her.

In her bedroom she donned trousers, appropriate for a seven-p.m. dinner. She added a white shirt and a white jumper. Then, collecting her torch, she set off for the McEldoo home at a few minutes before seven.

Hettie served a dinner of good, home cooked fare, chicken stew and biscuits, accompanied by a glass of Harp lager. It was all wonderful.

To Joanna, it felt like a family gathering. She

enjoyed the easy bantering between Mr. and Mrs. Mac. She didn't say much during the meal, but when tea and sweets were served, she brought the subject around to market day.

"Tell me what to expect tomorrow," she requested.

Hettie grinned and said, "Well I can't promise that Mr. Lewis will be there. I think that's what you're asking."

"Guilty," Jo admitted. "But what's the market like? I do want to know."

Hettie added tea to her own cup and to Joanna's. Horace took the hint and left the table. His wife began: "It'll be crowded, for sure. Folks from nearby villages and towns bring their wares to sell. Women and men from the countryside bring homemade food and goods. There'll be no shops open in the morning, but some shops will be having outdoor sales. By afternoon the village returns to normal."

Joanna was quiet, trying to take in all Hettie had told her.

Then, "I think it sounds wonderful. All these people milling around." She quietly considered the whole scenario, then admitted, "It would be easy to miss someone."

Hettie smiled sympathetically. "It would indeed, my dear," she added. "But you get a good night's sleep. We'll spend as much time there as you like. If he's there, we'll find him."

Joanna wakened early the next morning. She washed and dressed quickly to drive to the

McEldoo home and collect Hettie at seven a.m. The two ladies laughed and chatted on the two-mile drive west to the village proper. She had no trouble finding a parking place, thanks to her early arrival.

The morning mist was lifting, but still the air was damp. Joanna and Hettie pulled their woolen jumpers over their shoulders and set off to see what they could find.

Hettie, of course, knew many people there and stopped to chat with each one. She introduced Jo to everyone and more conversation ensued.

Eventually they came to the livestock area. Joanna was surprised to see this at market day, but she was fascinated by young bulls being auctioned, as well as heifers, sheep and chickens. She was so absorbed in this endeavor that she startled when Hettie nudged her arm. She jumped and shouted, "What!"

Hettie shushed her, then said, "Look over there, next to the ponies."

Joanna looked where she was directed and saw a dark-haired man talking to the horse's owner. "What about him?" she whispered.

The man turned to leave. Hettie sent a polite wave his way. He nodded in return. Then he saw Joanna.

She knew she was being studied. After a long moment, he nodded and smiled at her. Then he walked away.

"Was that Tony Lewis?" Joanna knew he was.

And Hettie chuckled, "In the flesh."

"But he wasn't close enough for me to get a good look at him," Jo protested.

"Don't worry," Hettie chuckled. "He got a good look at you."

Chapter 11

In the ensuing days, Joanna settled into a comfortable routine. Once the morning mist had lifted and the sun dared to show its face, she gathered her garden tools and began the work of clearing the stone path again.

Occasionally her thoughts would wander and she would find herself reflecting on past days. She remembered the fulfillment of singing, of being onstage or at a microphone and letting herself own the emotion of the music, feeling splendid. She remembered singing duets with her father, for John Whitfield had been well known as an accomplished baritone.

The wistful memories always brought her gardening to a halt, but before long Horace McEldoo would show up to help. Some days Hettie would come later and bring a picnic lunch with her. There were days when Hettie wasn't available. Horace would bring a basket of snacks with him. Always there was a bottle of Harp lager for him and a Coca-Cola for Joanna.

She walked inside the circle wondering what to plant there, and soon realized that she was feeling a strong, protective energy coming up from the earth.

Instinctively she knew that she wanted an oak tree there as a symbol of strength and purity. A startling flash of memory occurred, regarding her mother teaching her something to do with Druids and how they honored the oak tree.

Joanna was disturbed by this memory. Why now? Why here, in this place? It did seem that her recollections of her mother were of an "other worldly" nature. She'd been taught about the power of nature, of trees and plants, herbs and flowers. But other children had called her 'Spooky' when she told them of her lessons, so she kept the knowledge to herself. Gradually she spent more and more time with her peers, leaving less and less time with her mother. Her mother died when Joanna was ten years old and her teachings were presumably forgotten. Until now.

She would go to the market the next Wednesday and look for a nursery man with an oak tree to sell.

On the next market day, Joanna was up, dressed, and in her Morris before seven a.m. This would be her first time to visit the market alone. Putting her car in gear, she headed west on the 'B' road to Maiden's Heath.

She found a parking place just outside the village center. Today, on her own, she wanted to see everything there. Wearing her woolen jumper and carrying a very large tote bag, she set out.

In the center of the town square were the stands displaying homemade goods and foods made by local housewives. Bakers brought breads, scones, raisin cakes, and meat pies. Seamstresses showed denim shirts, plaid skirts and kilts, wool jackets, along with pristine white communion dresses and pictures of wedding dresses they could make to order.

There were stands with embroidered table cloths, pillow cases, and lace doilies of various sizes. Knitters brought socks, mittens, caps, and jumpers. Lots of people from other nearby villages were there to purchase these wares.

As Joanna walked the makeshift pathways in and around stands, she noticed a small girl sitting on the grass next to her father's barrels of produce. The child was overseeing a laundry basket which contained three squirming gray bundles of fur. Upon closer inspection, Jo determined that the furry bundles were kittens.

Jo knelt beside the child and asked if she could pick up one of the kitties

She removed her thumb from her mouth long cnough to say, "Ask me Da".

Her Da tipped his straw hat and greeted Joanna saying, "G'mornn'. You must be the lady livin' in the cottage by the heath."

She hadn't thought about her cottage being so near the heath, but as she mulled over the idea, she saw how that was possible. The wooded area at the bottom of her property wasn't nearly as dense as the rest of the forest, and the heath lay just beyond that.

"I am shc," Jo said, smiling, happy to have this recognition. "I am Joanna Whitfield. And I need a kitten." She was speaking as much to the thumb sucking child as to the girl's Da. She had no idea what to do with a kitten but she knew that Mr. Mac did. His old cat had wandered off and he would be happy to have a young one.

The farmer laughed. He declared that Joanna would have to convince Sally, his daughter to part with one. It wouldn't be easy.

Joanna knelt, smiled at Sally and in a sweet voice asked, "Sally, may I have one of you kittens?"

Sally shook her head 'no'.

Her father reached over and pulled her thumb from her mouth. "Answer the lady right!" he ordered.

Indignant, Sally shouted in her childish brogue "No! Ya con't have one! They is all mine!"

So resolute was the refusal that Joanna thought it useless to argue. And the farmer didn't intervene on her behalf, not a first. However, when Jo stood up to leave, he related an idea, "Maybe if you offer her some money - - -," he suggested. "I'll bet a shilling would buy your choice of them."

But Joanna had a different purchase price in mind. She got closer to Sally and bent down to whisper in her ear, "I will give you ten pennies for one kitten. You may choose the kitty for me and you may give him a name."

Sally popped her soppy wet thumb from her mouth and happily chortled, "Ten pennies? Goodie!"

"Which one shall it be?" Jo asked.

"Hmm," Sally pondered. "Take him," she said,

indicating the smallest of the three baby felines, a scrawny gray tabby with two white paws. "I name him Wilfred."

"Wilfred it is," Joanna agreed, as she picked up her furry purchase. She asked Sally "what would be the best way to carry him?"

"Put 'em in yer pocket," Sally instructed.

Indeed, the pitiful, forlorn kitten did fit right in the pocket of Jo's jumper.

Chapter 12

With Wilfred snuggled safely in her pocket, Joanna set off to find a nurseryman. After wandering up one lane and down another, she finally spied a man pruning shrubs that he hoped to sell. Reasoning that a man selling shrubs might also have trees available, she walked up to him.

The nurseryman had many young trees to sell. He had a plethora of fruit trees to offer and he tried to interest Joanna in them, but his efforts were in vain. She intended to purchase an oak tree. Nothing else would do. However, there was just one oak. It was spindly and looked to be weak, but it was the only one. It was barely three feet tall, but the nurseryman assured her that it had an adequate root ball.

The entire time Jo talked with the man; the kitten tried to escape. She had to keep her left hand on the feline in her left pocket or the curious Wilfred would climb up her sleeve. She suspected he was hungry or thirsty or both.

"How can I possibly carry a tree to my auto with only one hand?" She asked aloud, hoping the nurseryman would offer to carry it for her.

"Hmmm," the man muttered as he rubbed his

whiskered chin with his right forefinger and thumb. "I've got an idea!" he exclaimed. He took her tote bag and lowered the tree's root ball into it. He put the bag's handle in Jo's right hand, then arranged the scrawny trunk so it leaned on her right shoulder. He seemed very pleased with himself.

As she turned to walk away, the man bid her to wait. He instructed her to look to her left. She did so, but asked why.

"All the while we've been talking, a young lady has been sneaking peeks at you from behind the birch tree," the man told her.

Joanna continued to look in that direction and soon a black-haired young woman stepped boldly in view. The spy was Lily.

Joanna stood absolutely still, staring at Lily. *Why is she here?* Joanna thought. She couldn't deny the feeling of apprehension that was welling in her chest. She knew that if Lily was here, Moraig Dunne couldn' be far away.

At first, neither woman moved. Then, ever so slightly, Lily raised her right arm. With her right hand she beckoned Joanna to come nearer, a motion so small as to be easily missed. In fact, Joanna wasn't sure she saw the summon gesture until Lily repeated it.

With hesitant steps Joanna came closer to Lily. When she was but an arm's length from her, Lily turned abruptly and darted further away, then reeled around and faced Joanna again, beckoning.

"Oh hell!" Jo shouted. She tried to hurry her pace,

but the oak tree kept bouncing on her shoulder. Errant leaves clung to her hair. Wilfred was being rambunctious and climbed up her arm and scratched her neck.

Joanna suspected what she would find at the end of the 'cat and mouse' chase and she was right. Lily ran to a stand that Joanna had missed. And there was Moraig, standing vigilantly among hanging bunches of herbs and flowers.

Joanna had never seen so many different herbs. They were of every possible shade of green, from silvery to almost blue. Their combined aromas were heady and overwhelming, almost dizzying. She could identify dill and lavender. The rest were a mystery.

When she could no longer avoid it, Joanna turned to Moraig and acknowledged her. "Your herbs and flowers are the best I've ever seen," she said. She proceeded as Moraig said the names of many of them and of what use they were, all the while trying to control the tremor of her voice. Joanna was uncomfortable and she feared that Moraig knew it.

Finally, Moraig said, "I meant to thank ya fer the lift t'other day. Lily is delicate. It's no good fer her to get wet like that."

At hearing her name, Lily walked closer to Joanna, a hint of a smile on her face. Lily studied Joanna's hair and a flush of recognition appeared in her expression. Moraig's displeasure was immediate as she scolded Lily, ordering her away.

Joanna smiled at the girl, then responded to Moraig.

In her most courteous voice she said, "Lily wasn't bothering me in the least. As to the ride, well I couldn't let two women walk in that deluge. Anyone would have done the same."

There followed an uncomfortable silence. Though just a minute or so long, it unnerved Joanna. She felt she was being scrutinized by Moraig. Joanna knew she was no match for this woman. In a battle of will, Moraig would win.

Joanna's face became hot and red as she tried to think of how she could flee this situation. In desperation she picked up a small glass jar containing white cream. The label on the jar identified it as a moisturizer. "How much is this," she asked Moraig, trying not to show how anxious she was.

Moraig was cunning in her reply, not quite smiling as she said, "For you miss? I think that for one pound I could sell you that cream and this bunch of lavender and this pot of heather."

Joanna thought a pound for this escape route wasn't too much to pay. She quietly gave Moraig the required sum, shoved the jar of moisturizer into her purse, the pot of heather into her tote alongside the tree root ball. The sprigs of lavender she tucked into the waistband of her skirt. So armed, she set out to make her way back to her Morris, then to home.

Chapter 13

She had only taken about twenty steps when she collided with a man who was walking backwards while bidding farewell to another man. He collided with her, but she was already distracted by Wilfred trying to escape. She tried to apologize, but her brief bits of sputter didn't quite do it.

"Sorry - - - so sorry - - - damned tree - - - and the kitten won't behave - - - Wasn't watching - - -."

The gentleman didn't try to hold back from laughing. It overtook him; the whooping and guffaws were merciless. When she looked up to protest, he turned to face her. To her chagrin, her interrupter was Tony Lewis.

She was awestruck. No more words would come from her mouth, but her thoughts were pitiful: I *look terrible! A stupid mess! The tree! The cat!*

He was sympathetic to her struggle, and though a muffled chuckle occasionally came to the fore, he offered his assistance. "May I help you Miss Whitfield?" He asked as he removed the burden of the tree from her.

As she freed the kitten's claws from her skin and

jumper, she managed a quick smile and brief eye contact. Rather abruptly she asked, "How do you know my name?"

He helped her to the Morris before answering her question. As he cached the tree root ball in the auto's boot he said, "My darling, everyone in Maiden's Heath knows who you are. You started an account in the post office and the clerk passed your name to his family, etc."

He continued, "I'm probably the only person here who knows that you are a wonderful soprano as well as a beautiful woman."

"How do you know that I sing?" she was delightfully surprised.

"I heard you and your father sing with the symphony a few years ago, a lovely performance. And you know who I am, don't you?"

She blushed as she acknowledged him and his reputation in music.

"Alas," he said, checking his watch, "I don't have time to chat further. But let me take you to dinner tomorrow night. Seven o'clock at the Rook and Crown?"

She nodded enthusiastically and managed a faint, "I'd like that," and watched as he walked to his own vehicle. He turned and waved to her on the way.

She thought him the most charismatic man she'd ever met.

When she arrived home, she found Mr. Mac working

hard to eliminate more weeds from her stone path. He tipped his cap and greeted her, asking where she'd been.

"At the market," she said, struggling to keep the kitten from climbing out of her pocket again, while still balancing the tree against her shoulder.

Finally, she took the kitten from his lair and handed it to Mr. Mac.

"Well I'll be darned," he said, obviously delighted with the little animal.

"His name is Wilfred," Joanna informed him. "I paid a little girl ten pennies for him."

"He's a fine little fellow, but he's a wee bit scrawny."

Joanna could tell that Mr. Mac was very fond of this kitten already. "He's all yours. Let Mrs. Mac fatten him".

"I'll do just that," he said, "and thank you for Wilfred." Then he added, "Mrs. Mac will want to know where you got the heather. Not many folks grow it."

"Tell her it came from someone she told me to avoid."

The marketing, the encounter with Moraig Dune and abrupt meeting with Tony Lewis zapped Joanna's energy. At one o'clock that afternoon she decided to stop fighting the weariness and indulge in a nap.

She curled up on her parlor sofa, covered herself with a shawl and immediately fell asleep. She didn't stir until midafternoon when she wakened sensing she was not alone.

Joanna was careful to lie very still and not open her eyes. She willed strength to her sense of hearing, for she could detect faint whispering from more than one person. Soon she recognized the voices.

Letting her eyelids flutter a bit, she smiled as she heard Mr. Mac say, "See! Now we woke her."

Hettie Mac bent over and kissed Joanna lightly on her forehead apologizing for the interruption in her rest.

Jo sat up, stretched, yawned, and smiled at the couple, "I'm happy to see you," she assured them. "But why are you here?"

Chapter 14

"It's my doing, dear," Hettie Mac confessed. "Horace told me you were in contact with Moraig Dunne at the market. I worried that she might have done something harmful to you. Or sold you something harmful. I had to see for myself."

"The woman is sly," Hettie said. "She has no reason to dislike you, yet - - -."

Hettie and Horace looked intently at each other. Joanna couldn't read their expressions, but she was concerned nevertheless. "Something's going on," she stated. "What is it?"

"Well," said Horace, as he removed his cap and scratched his head, "Well we thought - - -"

Here his wife interrupted him. "We need to talk with you."

"Oh?" Joanna puzzled. "Let's go to the kitchen. I'll put the kettle on."

But Hettie quieted her, telling Joanna that she would do that. The young woman was to take a minute to fully wake up.

Joanna stretched again and smiled at Mr. Mac.

"There's no point in arguing with her," she laughed. He assured Jo that she was right.

A minute later Horace helped her up from her sofa and offered his arm as they made their way to the kitchen.

Mrs. Mac had three places set at the table. The tea kettle had just begun to steam as Joanna and Mr. Mac took their places. Hettie was unusually quiet as she poured their tea. She passed around a plate of buttered toast, then took her seat.

"We didn't mean to watch you sleep," Hettie began.

"No, we didn't," Horace concurred.

"We were struck by your looks," Hettie continued.

"My looks?"

"Asleep ya appeared more Scots than Brit," Mr. Mac explained.

"You really did, dear," his wife agreed. "Even now, with your hair wild and free. Your eyes as much green as blue in this light -- you have the look of a highland lass."

Joanna was pleased as she said, "that could be because my mother was a Scot. I have a strong resemblance to her and her family, as I have been told."

"And she had red hair?" Horace asked.

"She did indeed."

After a sip of tea, Hettie continued, "Her family

was Scots for generations back.”

“I believe so.”

Mr. Mac, busily chewing his toast and sipping tea, was nevertheless paying attention to the conversation. Abruptly, he asked, “When were you born?”

Joanna was curious about the reason for these questions, but she trusted the couple. “1937. The twenty-fifth day of October. Why do you ask?”

“I’ll get to that shortly,” he assured her. “When was your mother born?”

“Really?” The tenth day of November, 1916.” Mr. Mac wasn’t finished with his interrogation. “What was her name?” he persisted. His facial expression was absolutely serious.

“Her name was Rosemary. Really Mr. Mac!” Now Joanna was uncomfortable.

“Just a few more questions please?” Hettie McEldoo pleaded.

“You have a good reason for this?” Joanna asked.

“We do, Dear. I swear.”

Mr. Mac also assured her there were only two or three more things they needed to know.

Joanna acquiesced.

With a gentle voice he asked, “What was your mother’s maiden name?”

“Bowie. She was born Rosemary Bowie.”

He continued, “Born in Scotland of two Scots natives?”

"I'm almost certain that's true."

Hettie added, "Your mother was redhead? And her mother before her?" She was absolutely serious.

Alarmed, Joanna sat up straighter in her chair and pounded one fist on the kitchen table. "Yes! There are red haired women in every generation of my family. Now - - - please. What's this about?"

Mr. Mac cleared his throat and placed his teacup softly in its saucer. "Well, there was a prediction from Father Stephen that a new magic woman was about to emerge in this area and she has red hair. That's what the old priest said would happen. And her lineage was Scots."

Joanna was annoyed. "And this is me?" She posed.

"You fill the prophecy, Darling." This from Mrs. Mac.

Joanna was stunned. She couldn't process all this information and her mid was boggled, tending to believe that this was a colossal joke. "Tell me the whole story, Please. Who started this rumor? Does Moraig Dunne have any connection to this?"

"One question at a time," Horace said, chewing on his last bite of toast. He lifted the teapot and refilled his cup.

"You eat," his wife said. "I'll explain things to her." She took Joanna's hands in her own and began the story:

"You already know there are more witches in the

village than just Moraig and Lily. The rest of them avoid being out in public."

"But I need to go back in time, about twelve years at least. At the time the old priest lived here, in your house. You knew that."

Joanna nodded 'yes' and explained, saying, "I had a co-worker at the conservatory who was related to him. He was her great-uncle or something."

"What did she tell you about him?" Mrs. Mac asked.

Joanna shrugged her shoulders and replied, "Well, she said he was funny in the head."

Here Mr. Mac responded. "He was an odd fellow." Setting down his teacup, he readied himself to continue the story:

"He was from the monastery of St. Edmond. He was one of the brothers who burned the witches' holy ground and the circle you found. Some say it was his own guilt that made him crazy."

Here Hettie interrupted, "But he wasn't crazy. He certainly wasn't. No. He developed a sort of second sight."

Horace nodded in agreement. "He talked a lot about things that were to come. He had visions."

"Visions? Of what?" Joanna needed to know.

"Of things that other people didn't know," Horace revealed. "He talked about a red-haired girl who would show great powers. Another witch, perhaps, or maybe a girl with an extraordinary connection to the

Supreme Being. She would be a Scots woman, descended from a long line of healing women."

Hettie added, "He told us this one afternoon when he came into my kitchen as I was doing a card reading."

Surprised, Joanna interrupted, "Do you read cards for people?"

"Not for people, no," Hettie reputed. "I read for the future."

But Joanna was perplexed, claiming that she didn't understand.

"I can sense changes," Hettie said, "and my simple power isn't important now. We need to focus on you."

Silence followed. Joanna's thoughts were stirring so powerfully, the energy from them was palpable.

After a moment's pause, Joanna said, "Sorry. My head is beginning to hurt. I have a lot of thinking to do. I need to go upstairs and lie down."

Hettie and Horace left quietly.

Chapter 15

The next morning Joanna awoke with a headache. The conversation with the McEldoos and its importance to her weighed heavily on her mind as she carried out her morning routine.

As she lingered over a second cup of tea, she remembered that she had plans for the evening. She was astounded that her invitation from Tony Lewis could have been overshadowed by anything. But now she was happy, thrilled. She did a little dance as she washed and dried her breakfast dishes.

That evening, at ten minutes past seven, Joanna parked her Morris by the High Street kerb, just outside the Rook and Crown. She was late by design, not wanting to be seen waiting in the pub waiting for her date to show up. She entered through the door marked 'Lounge' and hoped that Tony Lewis wouldn't be waiting in the bar area instead. She was loath to walk into that 'men only' sacristy.

Stepping into the pub was like stepping back in time. She could imagine that two centuries ago horse drawn carriages stopped here. Travelers would have welcomed the pub's hospitality, for surely this pub had once been an inn. The wooden floors were well trod, with grooves and ruts worn where people had walked to the fireplace and to the stairs.

The fireplace was an enormous stone structure with an aperture large enough for a person to stand in. Joanna speculated that at a time before there was central heating, enormous fires were needed to heat inns such as this.

The ceiling was of a beautifully hammered tin. Its color was hidden by the residue of smoke from two hundred years' worth of pipes, cigars and cigarettes. Indeed, there were a number of people smoking there right now.

He saw her first. He left his table and walked to her. She couldn't take a step.

He was a man of perhaps forty-five years of age. She judged his height to be about five feet nine inches tall, just a couple inches taller than herself. He wasn't handsome, but he certainly wasn't ugly.

She found herself acutely aware of the texture of his skin. Her nostrils flared as she breathed in his scent, a combination of a woodsy smelling soap, pipe tobacco and some incredible male essence that was just him.

In the seconds it took for her senses to be completely saturated with this man, she was being mesmerized by his eyes, incredibly blue eyes that smiled knowingly into hers. She knew that he knew everything she was thinking.

Her face flushed with excitement as she stammered, "I'm so happy to see you!"

He placed his right hand on the small of her back and guided Joanna to the table he had reserved, gently escorting her to her seat.

The effect of his touch was more stirring to her blood than anything she had ever experienced. She felt her breasts swell. Her hips nearly swayed as she walked the few steps to her chair.

He helped her with the chair, then let his hand gently touch her hair as he walked around to his own seat. Joanna could scarcely breathe. Her eyes were wide and her heart was racing as he sat down directly opposite her.

When they made eye contact, she blushed like a thirteen-year old child, but she couldn't look away. She knew she was reacting to him like a silly school girl, but she was no longer a girl and he was certainly not a boy. She felt powerless in his presence.

It was eleven p.m. when they left the Rook and Crown.

She unlocked her auto door and turned to face Tony; her lips ready for his kiss. He pulled her to him, tilting her face up to his. He lowered his lips slowly, gently to hers. The kiss was soft at first, but quickly became ardent, possessive. Joanna's passion responded instantly.

Their tongues explored each other's mouths for just a moment. Abruptly, Tony pushed her inches away. Seeing the question in her eyes, he touched his fingers to her face and quieted her alarm. He smiled at her lovingly and whispered, "You go home now. I may forget that I'm a gentleman."

Chapter 16

While Joanna was dining with Tony at the Rook and Crown, six women were assembled in Maven Scarlett's sanctuary. Moraig and Lily had been the last to arrive, as she had been tending to an ill woman from the village.

There were four candles lit, sitting just about in the center of the oak table. They provided a meager amount of light which kept the energy in the room subdued. Mother Maven presided; Goddess Aoefe was content, curled in Maven's lap.

The three other women sat silently with heads bowed, praying. Moraig remembered meeting them at this same place a fortnight ago. They were witches that were driven away a decade ago. Now Mother Maven had summoned them back.

One witch, the oldest, lifted her head and with eyes kept closed, extended her arms, hands palm up. Then her hands began a beckoning motion, summoning some unseen force to come, be with them.

Moraig was uneasy. She sat quietly in her own thoughts, but her thoughts were a jumble. There was something she wanted to tell the group, but she didn't know Mother's plan for the meeting.

She would wait, she decided, and see how the meeting evolved. Meanwhile, she hoped her suspicions were correct. She hadn't long to wait. As Maven Scarlett rose to standing, Lily smiled at her and at each woman present. Instinctively, Mother took Lily's two hands in her own. She returned Lily's smile and embraced her briefly. Then she talked about the reason for this assembly.

"Welcome, my sisters," she said. "There's been something on my mind since we last met. I've been sensing that another woman like us is in the area. A magic woman, a benevolent woman, but powerful, just the same."

She paused, thinking, searching the space and atmosphere for connection. She spoke no words, but the vibration from her energy could be felt by all present. The very air trembled.

Opening her eyes, Maven continued. "I can feel her innocence. But trouble is coming. I am sure of it. It may involve us."

A pause, then, "Surely someone else has sensed her presence."

Moraig didn't hesitate. First, she asked for permission to speak. With that granted, she began.

"Remember Father Stephen? He lived in Rose Cottage, the house near the heath. His mental faculties were failing him during his last few years there, after his fellow Brothers burned his garden and our heath."

Mother Maven acknowledged knowing of the

priest, as did the others in the room.

Moraig continued, "One of his predictions was that a young, red-haired woman of Scots lineage would move into the cottage. He said that her energy would become powerful, once she solved the mystery of her life."

The oldest of the three showed some recognition of this story. Her face showed concern. She encouraged Moraig to continue her story.

"Well," Moraig resumed, "there is now a red-haired young woman living in that house. I've been near her twice. Her energy was stronger the second time than the first."

Maven asked, "Do you know her name?"

"I do. She is Joanna Whitfield."

Maven considered that for a moment, then added, "Whitfield isn't a Scottish name." another pause, then, "I get the feeling that her mother's family is Scottish. And probably red-haired. How can we learn more about her?"

Moraig offered, "The McEldoos know her. So does Tony Lewis. But I wouldn't ask him anything, ever."

"Do you still have all that hatred for him?" Maven Scarlett asked. "It's time to let go of that ill will."

Moraig made no reply so Mother Maven continued, "How are our friends, the McEldoos?"

"I don't have much contact with them," Moraig confessed. "But I do have three red hairs from

Joanna's head. They may tell me something."

At seeing the shocked expression on her leader's face, the guilty woman tried to defend herself, saying, "Lily plucked them from her head. I took them and hid them for safe keeping."

Mother Scarlett was clearly disturbed by this. "Why do they need 'safe keeping'? We don't cast spells on people anymore, only to improve health or fertility."

The mother witch paused briefly. Her ice-blue eyes narrowed and she grew taller as she spoke. "What do you intend to do with those hairs, Sister Moraig?"

"Nothin'," she lied.

"Get rid of them. Gently. Let them lie in a bed of flowers. Don't harm them."

"I will, Mother." Moraig seemed contrite, but she was lying a second time. She even apologized for possessing the hairs.

Now during this unpleasant exchange, neither woman gave a thought to Lily. While the girl never said a word, she did have some limited understanding of them. She also had memory of plucking red hairs from that lady in the car and giving them to her grandmother. And now her grandmother was upset. Mother Maven was upset too, and it had something to do with these hairs. In her limited ability to comprehend, Lily felt bad, as though she was at fault. She sat with her head down and tried not to hear anymore.

Moraig remained quiet as the women were served tea. The others were talking among themselves, remembering how strong the coven had been before the Christian Brothers decimated their holy land.

The eldest woman introduced herself as Sister Bridget and announced that she was originally from Scotland. Addressing the group, she related that she had known a family of red-haired witches when she was a child. "My family was from the west coast," she offered.

Moraig asked Sister Bridget if she remembered the family's name, but to no avail.

However, Sister Bridget continued, "Give me some time to reflect, Sister Moraig. I have a chant that I use for memory. Give me a few days to try."

This brought a smile to Moraig's face. Indeed, she was so pleased that she didn't notice Mother Scarlett studying her as she chatted with the others.

Chapter 17

A few days went by before Joanna and the McEldoo couple met again. She let the garden clearing come to a halt. She had other things to think about. Foremost in her mind was Tony Lewis and why she hadn't heard from him.

Thinking back to what the McEldoos told her, she swore she'd never heard of the women in her family being healing women or possessing other energies. Yet it was familiar to her, stored away back in her brain, further back than any other childhood memory. The idea sparked a flame that was dimly lit, yet wouldn't go away.

She spent Thursday and Friday at the public library, researching every book that had mention of witchcraft in Scotland. What she found referred to events in the past, none more recent than the eighteenth century.

She tried to trace her ancestry on her mother's side, but to no avail. Her father's line had been easy. Whitfield was common enough, though the name had changed over time. A century ago, Whitefield was the usual spelling. A century before that the name was Whytefelde.

But the female line of her family was nearly impossible to trace. Her mother's father's surname was Bowie; that she knew as her mother's maiden name was Bowie. But that grandmother's maiden name was a mystery to her.

Or was it?

Joanna had vague memories of herself and her mother visiting relatives in Scotland, in the village of Onich to be exact. Funny how that name had stayed with her. She couldn't have been more than four or five years of age, but vaguely, deep in some cobwebby crevice of her brain, she could recall a chilly morning there. She was at her aunt's table near the fireplace and playing with her dollies while her Ma and Auntie Elspeth talked quietly.

Elspeth was younger than her mother, Jo was sure. In her memory she recalled her auntie as being still like a girl. If Jo had been five years old then, her mother would have been about twenty-five or twenty-six. Auntie was perhaps twenty.

Jo hadn't seen her auntie since then. World War II had interfered with train travel. Jo's father, older than his wife by ten years, didn't get called up for duty, but he was active with the local civil authority. Her mother developed polio early in 1945 and succumbed to it in 1947.

Auntie Elspeth was forgotten. Until now.

Jo knew she had to go to Scotland. She had to find her aunt. Elspeth may have married; if so, her name would no longer be Bowie. She may not be easily found. But Jo had to try.

Jo and her mother had visited Elspeth at her home

in the village of Onich. This village sat on an inlet on the west coast of Scotland, not far from Ben Nevis, the highest mountain in the British Isles. Rosemary, Elspeth and Joanna packed a basket of food one day and had a picnic lunch near the mountain.

She remembered lying in a grassy spot and looking as straight up as she could, trying to see the top of the mountain. However, Elspeth explained that the mountain was so high, the top was always in the clouds. It could not be seen.

Her memories were so vivid, she marveled at their clarity. It had been more than twenty years since her visit to her auntie, but Joanna was sure she would recognize Elspeth when she saw her again.

Not 'if' she saw her, but 'when'.

She would leave tomorrow and drive to London where she would stay overnight at a B&B'. The next day she would take an express train to Glasgow, Scotland. From there she would hop another train to Fort William where she would find lodgings and rent a car. She knew the way as though she traveled this route frequently.

Checking her watch and finding it near tea time, she decided to invite herself to the McAdoo's house for the repast. She ran across her back lawn paying no attention to the half-uncovered pathway and hurried to the kitchen door of Hettie and Horace's house.

Without first knocking she opened the kitchen door and saw Mrs. Mac setting the table for tea, Jo shouted in, "Better set three places. I'm staying for a bit."

Hettie reached out and grabbed Joanna in a bosomy

bear hug. "I'm so happy to see you!" She exclaimed and kissed her captive on the cheek. She called for her husband and when Horace came to the kitchen and saw Joanna there, he was delighted too.

"We feared we scared you away," he said, apologetically.

"Well, you did surprise me," Jo admitted.

"We threw too much at you," Hettie said.

"But it's alright," Joanna assured them. "You stirred memories that I didn't know I had. I remember my mother's sister, Elspeth Bowie, who lived in Onich, near Ben Nevis. I'm going there tomorrow."

The McEldoos said nothing at first. Hettie looked as though she was ready to protest, but Joanna stopped her. "Don't bother yourself," she insisted. "I have my itinerary planned."

"Is your aunt still in Onich," Hettie questioned. "How will you find her?"

"I'll ask around. Besides, there may be more Bowies there. Surely someone remembers her."

"Can you ring us occasionally?" Hettie asked

"I'll certainly try. And speaking of ringing up, I have an important call to make this evening. I must run. But oh! Please check on my oak tree while I'm gone! Please!"

Chapter 18

Joanna decided to ring up Tony Lewis at eight that evening. She had expected him to call her, because their dinner date had been so wonderful. She wanted to talk to him again, before her trip north.

She hurried home from the McEldoos in time to collect her thoughts about Tony. She was drawn to him as she had never been drawn to any other man. She was in danger of losing herself completely to him and she didn't care.

But did he feel the same about her? She was certain he did when they kissed goodnight, yet she hadn't heard from him since. He hadn't phoned though it had been a few days.

The abrupt intrusion of the jangling phone shook Joanna from contemplation. She grabbed up the receiver and demanded, "Who's calling?"

She was rewarded by the deep, male voice on the other end responding, "Hello beautiful."

"Tony!" she squealed with delight. "I was just going to ring you!" She was incapable of holding anything back from this man.

She confessed, "It's wonderful to hear your voice.

"Ah, my beautiful darling. I called to tell you that I'm going away for a fortnight, but now I want to see you," he admitted, in a voice so husky she knew what he was thinking.

She asked him to come to her and he said, "Yes." She ran upstairs to her bathroom and freshened her body. She was back down at the door when his Mercedes pulled into her driveway. She let him get inside the house before she reached for him. They embraced and kissed deeply.

She heard herself making sounds that she had never produced before, something between a whimper and a moan. He knew it was time and took her upstairs, holding her tight to him with his arm around her waist, kissing her face all the way.

They tore off each other's clothes, first shirts, then her bra. He pushed her slacks down off her hips as he stepped out of his own trousers. They fell onto her bed, pressing their naked bodies together. Immediately she wrapped her legs around his hips. They made love with great passion and hunger, each giving and taking.

After completion, she wouldn't let go of him. Tony lay with his face in her hair, declaring his love for her over and over again.

When tears escaped her eyes and trickled down her face to the pillow, Joanna assured him they were an expression of her being happier than she'd ever been.

They slept for a short while. Tony wakened first, still resting in her arms. He raised to a semi-sitting position and as he did, noticed an open suitcase on the floor. It was partly filled with clothes.

He watched her face as she opened her eyes and smiled lovingly at him. "Are you going away too?" He asked.

"I am," she admitted as she stretched her body luxuriously. "I'm going to Scotland to find my aunt, Elspeth Bowie."

"Find her?" he queried. "Is she lost?"

"No, no," she assured him. "Let me tell you the whole story."

"There's a story?"

"Indeed, there is. You see, my neighbors, the McEldoos, knew the old priest that lived in this house. Now, you know there's a coven of witches in Maiden's Heath."

"Where is this leading?" he asked, not hiding the wariness in his voice.

"The McEldoos told me that the old priest angered the coven and guilt changed his mental status. He made predictions, talked about things to come."

"Balderdash!" Was Tony's impatient reply.

"Please listen," she implored. "Then, the McEldoos told me that the priest predicted a magic woman would come to inhabit Rose cottage. And she would have red hair and be of Scots lineage."

"So?" He demanded, angrily.

"So, I have red hair and my mother was a Scot."

"Surely you don't place any credence into the imaginings of a mad, old man!" He insisted.

Defensively, Joanna retorted, "The McEldoos believed him. And I am curious enough that I'm going to Scotland tomorrow. I believe I have an aunt still there and I'm going to find her. And I'll ask Auntie Elspeth all about my mother's family, if they were magic or witches or whatever."

She was breathing heavily by the time she finished her rebuttal. She waited for his reply.

Tony's response came in a very hushed tone. He pleaded, "Don't go."

"Why on earth not?" she questioned.

"You could get into serious trouble with the coven here," he warned.

"I've already been advised to stay away from Moraig Dunne. Hettie McEldoo says the others aren't dangerous. They prefer to keep to themselves. And I may find it is all 'balderdash'. Or perhaps I won't be able to find Aunt Elspeth. But I want to try."

Tony sighed deeply, knowing he couldn't change her mind. He asked, "How long will you be gone?"

"I don't know. At least a week, I think. Less than a fortnight."

"I'll be gone a fortnight," he said.

"Where are you going?" Joanna asked, softly.

"It's alright. I made these plans long ago. I'm going to the U.S. of A., Indiana, to be exact. Hanover College has asked me to present a week long seminar on composing."

She nodded in comprehension, confirming, "And

you leave tomorrow?"

"I do. I'll stay at the hotel at Gatwick tonight. My flight leaves at ten in the morning."

They were silent for a brief time, but their thoughts were similar; *Will he forget me?* She worried. *Will she think I was a mistake?* He feared.

Finally, he spoke. "Let's agree to something, when we return home we'll start again. We'll have dinner at the Rook again. Reintroduce ourselves and build from there."

"Yes, yes, yes!" She cried, pulling him close and kissing him lovingly. "We'll fall in love all over again."

She watched as his Mercedes drove away, then hurried up the stairs and back to bed. As she hoped, she found the bed sheets still warm and smelling of him. She pulled the covers tight around her to be surrounded by his scent. It was almost like falling asleep in his arms.

Chapter 19

Early the next morning Joanna rang up the music conservatory where her friends Nicholas and Ellen still worked. She was able to connect with Nicholas and asked him to make a reservation for her at a two-star hotel that was nearby. She would be in London mid-afternoon and needed lodgings for just one night.

He suggested they meet for dinner and he would invite Ellen also. She agreed, rang off and finished packing. She thought that dinner with the two of them might be uncomfortable, except that after last night with Tony she wouldn't care what they said or how chummy they were. Her mind would be focused on the man she loved.

At noon she tossed her bags into the Morris and set off for the two-hour drive to her old neighborhood. Driving the M25 always made her tense, but she could do it, she knew. She went straight to Cornwall House and thanked God there was a parking area in front of the hotel B&B.

She found the hotel's reception area easily and thanked God again, for her room was on the ground floor; no steps to climb while carrying luggage. Her room was not grand, but it was clean and 'en suite'.

At seven p.m. she left her room and walked one very long block to the pub where her friends would be waiting. She spotted them easily, sitting quite close to each other at a corner table in the lounge. They greeted her enthusiastically.

They each ordered Beef and Guinness pie and had pints of Guinness to drink. They congratulated Joanna on how well she looked.

"Country air," she explained, because she knew they expected to hear it.

Ellen smiled broadly and bragged, "Well we have news to tell you."

"Oh?" Jo asked, as she noticed Nicholas' face turning red.

Ellen was exalted with excitement. "We are engaged to be married!" She squealed. And as she announced her success, she flashed her left hand before Joanna's face, revealing a huge diamond on a white gold band. "I told him nothing smaller than two carats!"

Jo's eyes quickly darted to Nicholas, but he wouldn't make the connection. The diamond was four times as large as the one he'd given Joanna. However, she was readily able to congratulate them both. She had Tony.

Later, back in her room and preparing for bed, she thought a lot about her trip planned for the next day. The train ride to Glasgow would take about six hours for it was a 'local' and would make several stops. Discharging riders and taking on new ones ate up a lot off travel time

From Glasgow she would hop a train to Fort William, a shorter ride. There she would find a 'B&B' and spend the night. The next morning, she would hire an auto and drive to Onich.

The train to Glasgow left from London's Eustace Station. It was a pleasant enough ride, if a bit long. At about noon Joanna heard the unmistakable rumble of a refreshment cart being pushed up the center aisle. Soon she could hear the porter chanting his wares. "Coffee, soda, water, sandwiches, biscuits." He recited this list in rhythm with the trains' movement, a constant 'ba boomp, ba boom. She thought the porter and the train worked as one.

Joanna ordered coffee and a ham sandwich. The coffee wasn't hot and the sandwich wasn't fresh, but she ate it anyway. She didn't know when more food would be available.

Soon after, she felt sleepy. The train's rhythm was like a rocking chair and she succumbed to the gently swaying. She wakened more than an hour later with the need to find the W.C.. Soon after that, she arrived in Glasgow.

Chapter 20

Joanna scrambled to take her luggage from the train and get to the lift which led to the bridge that crossed above the tracks. There a second lift took her down to where the tracks took trains in a different direction. There she waited for the 5:30 p.m. train to Fort William.

She saw a small kiosk where she could buy another sandwich if she so chose. She dragged her luggage to the structure and found the same stale sandwiches. She actually saw green mold on the bread, so she chose a brownie wrapped in plastic and hard as stone. At least the coffee was good.

Time passed slowly. There were few other passengers waiting with her, but a young male student was friendly and helped her lift her luggage on board. She took a window seat, but the young gent went to the back of the car.

The ride to Fort William was two hours long. It was 7:30 p.m. when Joanna arrived there. Joanna had only to walk about one hundred feet from the train station to find a street where many homes sported 'B&B' signs. She knocked on the door of the first home she came to. She was met there by a late-middle-aged woman in a house dress and a very clean pinafore.

"Come in," the pleasant lady invited.

"I need accommodation for a few nights," Jo explained as she sat her suitcase down in the reception foyer.

"I have just the room for you. It's on the first floor, just up one flight of stairs."

The hostess extended her right arm to shake hands and introduced herself as Mrs. Grogan. "And your name?" She asked.

"I'm Joanna Whitfield. I live in Surrey."

Mrs. Grogan studied Joanna's face and stature for a moment, then pronounced, "You've a bit of the Scot in you." "What was your family name?"

"It was Bowie," Jo replied, but added, "I don't know if there are any family members still in Onich. That's what I'm here to find out."

Mrs. Grogan led the way to the room she had in mind for Joanna. It was clean and cozy, but no frills. Jo knew she would be fine without any extras, but would prefer a private lavatory. However, her landlady said that Jo would have to share the 'loo' with the young lady renting the room next door. Mrs. Grogan assured her there would be no problem; the other young woman was rarely in. And breakfast would be serviced between seven a.m. and eight a.m.

So, Joanna prepared for bed. She opened her window and was surprised at the coolness of the night air. She was reminded of how far north of London she was, and in the Grampian Mountains besides. She slept well.

The next morning at breakfast, she met her neighbor and lavatory-sharer. The young woman was cordial, but in a hurry, explaining she had to be at her secretarial job at eight-thirty.

Jo smiled and said that perhaps they would meet again that evening. However, her new acquaintance explained that she had another job; that evening she would be singing at a club. She'd be coming home late and would go directly to bed.

"Well, ta," Jo said as she gave a tiny wave of her hand and watched her neighbor leave. She wasn't sure she had even heard the woman's name.

When Mrs. Grogan came to clear the table, Joanna took the opportunity to ask about local auto hires. She was directed to walk a few blocks to a more commercial area. There she would find MacLeod's auto hire service. Soon after, she was motoring south in a compact red Ford. She took the A road, headed for Onich.

She found the scenery dramatic and breathtaking, with steep hillsides on her left and sloping grassy areas on the right that led down to Loch Linnhe and then to the Sea of the Hebrides.

"Hebrides," she murmured. The name resonated with her. Surely, she'd heard the name before, referring to the Hebrides Islands, but - - - the Sea of the Hebrides - - - the name touched something deep inside her.

Again, the image of her mother, Aunt Elspeth and her five-year-old self, sitting at the foot of Ben Nevis returned to her. But now a smattering of their conversation returned as well. They spoke of a sea whose full name she couldn't recall.

She knew she was quite close to Ben Nevis. Soon she saw the parking area that served it and she drove the Ford in. There were only two other autos parked there, for in the early mornings the mountain was heavily obscured by mist. It would be noon before many other autos arrived.

Joanna exited her auto and walked to a path which would take her to a humid, soggy, glen, overgrown with tall reeds and ferns. One had to walk through the glen to get to the mountain. She started on the path, cautiously at first, but feeling stronger with each step.

Soon she saw the terrain was changing, now dryer and rising little by little. She stopped and looked up into the mist. There she waited, as if expecting a message to come to her, for she sensed that the mountain was alive. She could feel its energy, as though it was feeding her.

She saw a flicker of sunlight poking through the mist. She didn't believe it at first for it was only midmorning and usually sunlight wasn't apparent until afternoon. But the light persisted and grew brighter. In the veiled rays of light, she saw flecks of green and white that a child would have recognized as fairy wings. They seemed to flutter around her body, insisting that she walk no further. Jo knew this was a sign that she should return to her quest.

Chapter 21

As Joanna entered the village of Onich she'd no idea where to park and began her search. She spotted a building that had a long porch and four tall columns supporting its roof. Deciding this might be the seat of official business that she needed, she found a nearby autopark and left her Ford there.

Approaching the porch, she saw a sign above a revolving door. The sign said "Tourist Information." *Just the thing,* Jo thought. However, to her dismay the door was unmovable. She tried to push it, then pull it, but it wouldn't turn. Then she saw the note posted on the wall beside the door that read, "Closed 11 a.m. to 1 p.m."

A bell in a church steeple ran eleven times. Joanna thought the employees must have locked the door a few minutes early, then snuck out the back door.

It seems I have two free hours, she thought. *I think I'll amble about Onich, see if anything jogs my memory.*

The first shop she visited was a clothing store. She walked in and soon saw a rack of child-sized kilts in various tartans.

Jo paused by them. She ran her fingertips gently down the pleats of a kilt of the Hunting Stewart tartan. It was beautiful in its green and red colors. She remembered wearing her own kilt, its coarse wool and how it scratched her legs when she danced in it.

Her mother had dressed her in a kilt often as she was growing up. She wore it for holidays and dancing competitions. Her dancing outfit consisted of the kilt, a green velvet vest and a long-sleeved white blouse that sported a large, front ruffle. She'd worn her costume when they'd visited Aunt Elspeth.

Like morning sun pushes away mist, some here-to-fore unacknowledged fog in her brain was lifting, allowing clear memories to enter. She recalled Elspeth as a spirited young woman making breakfast for her and her mother, the aroma of ham and sausages frying in a skillet over an open flame on the iron stove. Elspeth seemed to dance through the kitchen, as light as a fairy. And how she and her mother laughed as Elspeth made the meat float in the air before landing on their plates! Elspeth was magic and Joanna loved her.

Joanna was vaguely aware that she uttered something when a saleswoman approached her, offering assistance. She introduced herself as Mrs. Adams.

Joanna's face revealed her wonder. "I remember having a kilt when I was child," she explained. "It was green, but I don't think it was the Stewart." Turning to Mrs. Adams she asked, "Do you think you could help me find the right one?"

The woman smiled pleasantly and asked what clan name she should look under.

Joanna replied, "My mother's maiden name was Bowie."

"That's somewhere to start," the shop lady said. She retrieved a large, bound book from beneath a counter and began a search through it.

"If you don't mind me asking," Joanna ventured, "have you lived in Onich all your life?"

The woman said, "Nay miss. I came here as newlywed, five years ago. My husband is the pastor of that church up the road."

"Is he originally from here?" Joanna pursued.

"Nay miss. The presbytery moved us here when we were newlyweds, as I said. We're both from Glasgow."

With a hint of triumph in her voice Mrs. Adams announced, "Aha! I've found it. Bowie is a popular name on the islands."

"You mean the Hebrides?"

"Aye. I do. I found the Bowie name as a sept of Clan MacDonald. They wear the MacDonald tartan."

A short pause ensued, then Mrs. Adams added, "I believe you are entitled to wear the specific MacDonald of the Isles pattern, the Ancient Hunting," and she showed Jo a sample of the green tartan she'd worn.

"That's it!" Joanna proclaimed. "Oh Mrs. Adams! I must have one!"

"Can I have it delivered to my home in Surrey?" Jo hoped aloud. She was assured her request posed no problem.

Before she left the shop, Joanna had another question to ask. "Mrs. Adams, might there be an older person in the village who could remember the Bowie family? I might have an aunt, Elspeth Bowie, living here yet."

"There's an elderly woman, a Mrs. Shelley. Mrs. Helen Shelley, of the Historical Society. She might remember the family. She's in her nineties and I believe she's lived most of her life here."

Joanna was thrilled and urgently asked, "Where can I find her?"

Chapter 22

Mrs. Helen Shelley lived in a poorly maintained two story, frame house situated on a short, back street just off the High Street. The house may have been painted at some time in the past, but at present its color couldn't be determined. Though the day was chilly there was no smoke rising from the chimney. The dirty windows didn't reveal any evidence of life inside.

The street was named Shelley Way, probably because there were no other houses on it. Farmland began at the end of the street, but the land lay idle, no crops, no animals. It seemed to have been tilled a long time ago, then just forgotten.

Joanna rang the doorbell and heard chimes resonating inside the house. When this brought no response, she rang the bell again. Presently she heard the click of the lock as the deadbolt slid to its open position.

Inside the opened door stood a disturbing figure. A woman of sicky thinness faced Joanna. The two women studied each other for a moment that seemed endless. The woman stayed a few feet back from the open door, but Joanna could see that the skin on her face and arms was loose, sagging and of a deathly pallor. Lank stands of dim hair hung about the woman's face. Only her eyes showed life. They were pale, but definitely green. They stared at Joanna's face.

The woman was obviously weak and guarded. Joanna wondered if she had a debilitating illness. Or perhaps she was mentally infirm. It was a puzzle.

Joanna spoke first, saying, "I'm Joanna Whitfield."

Mrs. Shelley raised one thin hand to stop her from saying anything more. She asked, "What is your Scots family name?" The woman's voice was thin, but commanding.

"Bowie," Jo stated.

Mrs. Shelley continued to stare at Jo. Finally, she said, "You have that look about you."

She didn't invite Jo inside, nor did she ask Jo's purpose in being there, but continued, "Come back tomorrow, in the evening. She'll be here. She knew you were coming."

"Elspeth?"

"Tomorrow. Six p.m." Mrs. Shelley whispered as she closed the door.

The drive back to Fort William went by quickly because Joanna's mind was more focused on Mrs. Shelley then on the road. She was profoundly curious about her. Jo would ask Elspeth about her tomorrow. And how did Elspeth know she was coming to Onich? And why would she know this ghostly woman?

Joanna felt alone. She missed her home in Surrey

and the McEldoo couple. She missed her gardening, the discoveries on her property. She missed singing. She missed Tony Lewis. Tony. She didn't even know how to get in touch with him. But she could ring up Hettie and Horace. She'd call from the 'B&B' and give them her phone number. She would do it tonight.

Joanna arrived safely back in Fort William in late afternoon. Opening the B&B's door, she met Mrs. Grogan just inside. The Scots hostess smiled at Jo and welcomed her back with a hug.

"Aye, Dearie, you're here before the rain. Maybe you'll have dinner here with the few of us so you don't have to risk the weather?"

"No maybe about it," Joanna answered, "I'm in for the night. Oh, and I have a question. I must ask a favor."

"What can my Dearie need?" Mrs. Grogan asked.

"Well, I need to place a call this evening, if I may use your phone. The call will be long distance, to neighbors in Surrey."

Mrs. Grogan nodded and instructed, "Have the operator place the call and ask her to tell you the charge at the end. You pay me the amount. There'll be a fee for supper also."

"That's fine," Jo agreed. "One more thing. I'll need to stay an extra night, ok?"

"Right enough. Wait until after six to make your call. Rates are cheaper then. And dinner is at seven."

Chapter 23

At six p.m. Joanna checked with Mrs. Grogan again about using the telephone. Her hostess assured her that there was no imposition, just follow the instructions she was given.

So, Joanna dialed the operator and asked to be informed of the charges. Her call went through without a problem.

Horace McEldoo answered the phone in a distracted kind of voice. "McEldoo here. Who's callin'?"

"It's me, Mr. Mac! Jo!"

"Well I'll be darned," he said. Then, "Hold on while I get the missus. Hettie!"

"You don't have to shout," his wife scolded. She took the phone from his hand, mildly annoyed at being called away from her telly. "Who's there?" Hettie asked.

"It's me Joanna."

"Ah well, then." She moved the phone a bit away from her mouth and, speaking to her husband said, "It's Joanna."

Jo could hear him chuckling in the background.

She got the woman's attention by shouting, "Mrs. Mac! Mrs. Mac!"

There was reprimand in Hettie's voice as she answered, "I can hear you Joanna. No need to shout." Then, in a kinder tone she asked, "Where are you?"

"I'm at the Blue Moon B&B in Fort William. It's good to hear your voice."

"Likewise, my angel," Hettie responded. Then aside, she shouted to her husband, "Horace! Get a pencil and some paper. She's staying at the Blue --- what?"

Joanna repeated, "Blue Moon."

"Blue Moon B&B. In Fort William. Write that down, Horace." Then, "How long will you be there?"

Jo answered, "Two more nights after tonight, at least. Not certain."

"Any luck finding your auntie?"

"Yes," Jo admitted. "I have had some luck. I'll give you all the details when I get home."

"Fine, that's fine," Hettie agreed. In a more serious tone, she asked, "You've not run into any danger, have you?"

Joanna spoke quietly, "I met a strange woman, but I didn't feel I was in any danger. I don't want to discuss it over the phone."

Then, more cheerfully Jo asked, "How is everything in Maiden's Heath?"

Laughing, Hettie replied, "Just the same as you

left it three days ago."

"Oh, course it is," Jo realized. "But I have a favor to ask; two favors really."

"Ask away."

"Alright. For number one; please check on my new oak tree. It's been doing so well. I hope it doesn't miss me. And favor number two. I'm expecting a package to be delivered. I ordered a kilt in Onich. It had to be made to my measurements then mailed to my home. I'll probably get home before it arrives, but just in case - - - "

"No worries my girl, right Horace?"

Jo could hear Horace in the background agreeing with his wife saying, "Anything I can do to help."

Hettie paused before saying, "Now I have something to tell, or ask you, Joanna."

"Oh? Tell me."

"Earlier today Tony Lewis rang me up. He wanted to know if I'd heard from you. He left a phone number where he could be reached. He asked me to give it to you."

But Jo's response was, "No. I don't think so. I don't want the temptation to ring him up. Just tell him you heard from me and I'm fine."

"Why don't you want to phone him?" Hettie's voice was full of surprise.

"Because he didn't want me to make this trip. He'll scold me, perhaps get angry." A pause ensued, then, "He doesn't want me to develop magic powers.

He said the Maiden's Heath coven will be suspicious of me. Especially Moraig Dunne. I don't understand any of it."

"Then he hasn't told you," Hettie speculated.

"Told me what?"

Hettie knew she had misspoken. She tried to end the conversation by saying, "I shouldn't have said anything. It's not my place to - - -"

Joanna cut her off mid-sentence.

"Tell me Hettie! This isn't fair. Tell me!"

"Seeing as how you're insisting - - -"

"I AM insisting!"

"Alright," Hettie acquiesced. "You've met Lily. A beauty, isn't she. She's the image of her mother, Trilby. Well, Trilby was a spirited girl. She loved boys and they were drawn to her. She was about sixteen years old when Tony Lewis moved here. He was a young man, not a boy. He would have been about twenty-five."

"Any road, Trilby wouldn't stay away from him or his house. Rumor was, she snuck away during the night and was seen walking home before dawn. A few months later she was obviously pregnant. Moraig threatened to kill him."

"Now, again the rumors spread that Moraig tried to abort the baby, more than once. Trilby was sick all through the pregnancy and for several months after. She died about the time of Lily's first birthday."

"Silence ensued. Joanna knew what Hettie wasn't

saying: Tony was Lily's father.

Joanna whispered, "I have to go now. I must sit down."

She found a soft, upholstered chair in the guest lounge and sank into it. She was stunned. She wasn't aware of one clear thought going through her mind; there was a jumble of facts contradicting each other. She didn't know how to come to any conclusion, so she just let the storm rage on.

She was still in the chair at seven p.m. when Mrs. Grogan rang the dinner bell. Joanna was grateful for the interruption.

Chapter 24

At breakfast the next morning, Joanna was unusually quiet. Mrs. Grogan and the other guests were cordial to her, but she didn't invite conversation. She sat alone at a small table, apparently studying the scene outside the window.

She had slept poorly the night before. Her dreams were disturbing, a combination of the wraith -- like Helen Shelley beckoning her with a skeletal hand and arm, an evil glint in her pale, green eyes, and Moraig Dunne ready to behead Tony Lewis.

Her opinion of Tony had changed, she knew it. The truth of the relationship between him and the teenage daughter of Moraig Dunne was distasteful, to say the least.

What if the girl had thrown herself at him? How did she get into the house? He must have let her in - - into his house and into his bed. Hettie had insinuated that there was more than one occasion when Trilby was seen going home in the pre-dawn hours.

And he hadn't protected her from getting pregnant. What kind of man does that?

At five forty-five that evening, Joanna parked her rented Ford one block away from Mrs. Shelley's house.   She intended to wait until precisely six o'clock before knocking on Mrs. Shelley's door. Ordinary she wouldn't have thought that fifteen minutes early was rude, but she had never dealt with anyone like this woman. Jo would wait until precisely six p.m., as per her instructions.

While she waited, thoughts of Tony Lewis crept into her consciousness. She tried to replace those thoughts with questions about Aunt Elspeth and sometimes she was successful. She hoped her aunt would be happy to see her.

Still, she was in love with Tony. She remembered the night they became lovers and her body was stirred by the memory. But she didn't know how to reconcile his affair with Trilby Dunne.

Remembering to check her watch brought her back to the present situation.   The time was now five minutes before six, time to make a move.

Joanna got out of her auto slowly, buttoned her jacket as protection against the evening coolness and locked the auto door. She fixed the strap of her shoulder bag so it wouldn't slide off and walked slowly to Mrs. Shelley's house.

The house on Shelley Way looked like it had come alive Every window on the ground floor revealed light inside. Leaves on nearby tees had fully opened and were being gently rustled by a soft breeze. The entire area exuded warmth that had not been present the day before. Joanna could hardly believe the trans-formation.

The door opened with her first knock. Joanna

expected to see the pale creature she met yesterday. Instead, she was greeted by a tall, slender woman with long, lustrous auburn hair. Her green gown brought out the green in her eyes which sparkled with pleasure at seeing her niece. "Joanna! I've been waiting for you!"

"Oh, Aunt Elspeth. I'm so very happy to see you again."

Joanna thought she had never before seen as beautiful a woman. A light glowed around her body and Joanna recognized this as an aura. Immediately next to Elspeth was a thin rim of pink light. It faded into a halo of white which encircled her body. Joanna knew that this was the woman's energy, wonderful, healing, loving energy being revealed.

Jo entered the home, never taking her eyes off her aunt Abruptly, she wondered aloud, "Where is Helen Shelley?"

Elspeth's eyes twinkled as she teased, "I gave her the day off."

Jo's confusion was evident when she asked, "I don't understand. Isn't this her house?"

"Helen died years ago, it's my house now. She left it to me."

Shaking her head, Joanna asked, "Wasn't that Helen I met here yesterday?"

Mischievously, Elspeth instructed her to close her eyes. "For only a minute," she promised.

Jo did as she was bidden, and when she opened her eyes again, she saw the ancient specter of a woman she thought was Helen Shelley.   But Helen was wearing Elspeth's green dress.

Joanna blinked and in a tick of a moment Helen was gone. Aunt Elspeth was present again.

Joanna gasped and demanded, "How did you do that!"

Elspeth just hugged her niece and laughed, saying "One day your powers will outshine mine."

Chapter 25

Elspeth took Joanna by the hand and led her to a seat at the table. On the table sat a teapot, steam escaping from its spout. There were two cups, along with two saucers and two teaspoons. A plate held tiny cucumber sandwiches and sweet biscuits.

The women sat close to each other and held hands. Joanna's eyes filled with tears as she confessed, "I have so much to ask you."

Elspeth offered, "I think what you want is to know about your mother and our family. Am I right?"

"You know you are."

"Right. Rosemary was already seven years old when I was born. There was always just the two of us, none before and none between."

Jo said, "I remember her red hair. Was her mother, your mother, a redhead too?"

"She was indeed," Elspeth assured her. "You are the image of your mother and grandmother."

"Tell me about my grandmother," Jo asked.

"Well, she was Lizzie Beaton Bowie, she was both fragile and fierce, carefree and heavy burdened,"

Elspeth answered. "She was pretty, but it was the liveliness in her soul, the challenge in her confident nature that drew men to her."

"Where was she born?"

"On the Isle of Skye. In October, 1898," Elspeth stated. "She married there, an island man, James Bowie. He was quite a few years older than Lizzie."

"She used to laugh and say that he tried to tame her, but failed completely."

"Was she a magic woman?" Joanna needed to know.

"Was she a witch?"

"Lizzie Bowie, nee Beaton, was a green eyed, red-haired wonder. As was her mother, Mary Beaton. I'd say Lizzie was a white witch in her younger days." Elspeth closed her eyes. She was searching deep inside for a way to explain her mother's powers to Joanna. When she began, her eyes were no longer sparkling; they revealed her cautious, pensive mood.

"Lizzie was very powerful. Even as a young woman she understood herbs and how to use them. I remember watching her concoct tinctures and elixirs. She used to meditate, go within, before making her medicine. I knew not to disturb her during these times. Your mother would keep me busy in the house. Lizzie always meditated outdoors, in the garden. Actually, that's why they had to leave Skye."

"Why?" Joanna quizzed.

"The pastor of the Protestant church observed her one day. He asked his few parishioners about Lizzie and when he heard the words 'healing woman,' he called her a non-believer, a witch. The local doctor agreed.

"James feared for her life, as well as the lives of their daughters. He moved us all to Onich."

"All four of you," Joanna mused. But Elspeth contradicted her. She said, "Actually there were five. Mary Beaton came with them. She too had powers and was in danger."

"And Mary's husband?" Joanna asked, naively.

"Uh, let's just say that Lizzie never knew her father."

"Maybe that's why she was so inconsistent," Jo suggested. Then she added, "How old were you, everyone, when you moved?"

"Well, I was but six years old, so Rosemary would have been fourteen. Lizzie, just thirty or thirty-one. Mary, maybe fifty, not older. James -- I really don't know."

"So, Lizzie was only sixteen when my mother was born," Jo commented.

The ladies paused their conversation for tea and sandwiches. Jo realized she was weary and suspected that Elspeth must be, too. She said, "There's more I want to know, but I can come back another day if you need to rest."

"No," Elspeth said, "let's continue now. There's something I must do tomorrow. You need information about our powers and your own."

Chapter 26

"I do," Jo admitted. "Sometimes I know something and I don't know how I do. And there have been times when I knew something was coming, or going to happen. I have instincts. My mother told me to pay attention to them. It's like I feel I have some power, but I don't know what to with it or how to use it."

"That's what it was like for your mother. She wasn't extremely powerful for most other people, but her protective senses were strong for me, herself and you."

"Not every woman in our family has or had the same strength in powers. Mary Beaton for instance, was an awesome midwife. She had remedies for infertility; she could tell a girl when she was ripe enough to conceive; she knew the sex of each baby and was expert at helping with delivery. But that was her limit of power."

Here Joanna became alarmed. She asked crisply, "She didn't do abortions, did she?"

Elspeth sensed Jo's uneasiness. She again closed her eyes and briefly turned her gaze inward, remembering. Quickly she reassured Joanna. "No, I don't believe she did. Her practice was about bringing life, not ending it. Why are you so troubled?"

With a sigh, Joanna began her tale about the coven in Maiden's Heath, stating that she was told she had nothing to fear from the coven itself. It was Moraig Dunne she was afraid of.

Moraig, who made potions from herbs and performed abortions. Joanna told how she met Moraig and Lily and about subsequent interactions with them.

Joanna told Elspeth about Tony Lewis, how he was connected to Moraig and Lily and how her own feelings for him were conflicted. And she told Elspeth about her friends next door, Horace and Hettie McEldoo, and about the sacred circle on her property and the old priest who'd lived in her house.

Elspeth listened quietly and remained silent for a moment or two afterward, her eyes again closed. When she stirred, her eyes were a darker shade of green and she spoke very, very seriously: "Joanna, my dear girl. It is no accident that you sought me at this time. And I knew you were coming, but I didn't understand the dire need of your quest."

"Dire need?"

"Absolutely. You thought you were coming for information. You wanted to know more about your mother and her family. That's what I foresaw, too. But you have danger around you in Maiden's Heath."

"From Moraig Dunne and the coven," Joanna guessed.

"Not the coven. It is led by a magnificent woman,

a witch who has evolved over many decades. Maven Scarlett. I'd bet she's already aware of you."

"No, your danger is Moraig. And it involves your Tony Lewis, too."

Joanna asked reluctantly, "He will hurt me, won't he?"

Elspeth shook her head. "I don't sense any evil with his name. Maybe a problem, though."

Jo continued, "And the McEldoos?"

Elspeth was puzzled. "My senses tell me that they are like parents for you."

"That's how I feel about them," Jo admitted.

"They are the right people for this time in your life," was the answer. Then, "When do you plan to go home?"

"You mean to Surrey?"

"I do mean just that."

"I could go tomorrow," Jo realized.

"No!" Elspeth was adamant. "Wait until the day after," she insisted.

"If you think it best," Joanna agreed. "May I ask why?"

Elspeth shook her head 'no'. "All will be revealed quite soon. Your powers will manifest and soon. Don't be afraid to call on them."

"Like following my instincts?"

"Yes, but more protective."

“Will I ever see you again?” Jo asked.

“You will, I will be near you often. I may look different at times, but you will know me.”

Chapter 27

It was half past nine when Joanna arrived at the Blue Moon Bed and Breakfast. The door of the house was locked, but she rapped lightly and Mrs. Grogan promptly came to her rescue.

"Ah, you're here at last," Mrs. Grogan proclaimed. "I've been fretting about you."

Joanna smiled at this, but said, "Don't fret about me. I'm very independent and self-reliant." The women hugged like old friends.

Joanna admitted, "I am weary. And hungry."

She had no more than uttered the words than Mrs. Grogan was leading her to the dining table. "You sit down right here," the hostess said. "I've kept a little something for you."

"I've kept a plate of supper warm." Mrs. Grogan said, her voice trailing off as she entered her kitchen. She returned a moment late carrying a heavily laden tray of food.

"Here you are, my dear girl," she offered as she set a plate of roasted chicken and boiled potatoes on the table. There was also a carrot and parsnip mash, presented with a few sprigs of parsley.

"Eat it all, please," Mrs. Grogan instructed.

Joanna couldn't help smiling at Mrs. Grogan's motherly behavior. It made her think of Hettie McEldoo, whom she missed very much.

Joanna did indeed finish her plate and was sipping her tea when she became aware of the telephone ringing. She was about to call Mrs. Grogan from the kitchen when the woman appeared and passed her. She grabbed the receiver from its cradle and answered in an annoyed manner. Joanna could easily hear her part of the conversation.

"Blue Moon Bed and Breakfast!"

A pause, then, "Yes, I remember your previous call. Yes, she's here just now. I'll bring her to the phone."

"Joanna! This is for you!"

Expecting one of the McEldoos to answer, Jo said, "I didn't think you would call again. I'll be home day after tomorrow!"

But the response that came was a surprise. "This is Tony, darling. I've been worried about you. I didn't want you to go - - -"

Joanna cut him off. "Tony you have no right to prevent me from doing anything. For your information, this trip has been quite beneficial for me."

"What did you learn?" He demanded, completely unchastised.

"Nothing that I will tell you on the phone," she insisted. Then she remembered he was probably in the

U.S.A. "Where are you calling from?" she asked, a bit more relaxed.

"I'm still in America," he replied.

"Well I'm going home day after tomorrow, as I said," she reminded him.

"Hmm," he mused. "I'd planned to be gone a fortnight, but I'll be home in a couple days too. I need to see you."

His change of plans disturbed her. She immediately knew she wanted some days free of him, at home. "No," she said. "Don't come home that early just because of me."

"Why not!" he demanded.

"Because I need a few days to sort things out. You would be too much of a distraction."

There was a short period of silence. Finally, he acquiesced, saying, "Alright. I understand."

"Still friends?" she asked.

"At least that." he replied, and ended the call.

The rich baritone of his voice stirred her. His face, his touch, the feel of his body -- all were vivid in her memory. Aunt Elspeth was certain there was no evil in Tony, but how could she know. She had never met him. And his history with Moraig Dunne's daughter -- Elspeth had made no comment about that.

But Joanna's feelings for him had changed since knowing that he fathered Lily.

Still, Joanna admitted that Elspeth was incredibly

powerful. Jo could and would trust her aunt.

She made her way up to her room after thanking Mrs. Grogan sincerely for the meal. Her bed looked inviting, but Joanna thought it advisable to shower first. The shower drain was noisy. It sputtered as though it was choking and reminded her of her bathtub at home. Home. The word had a secure feeling to it.

Tomorrow she would ascertain her train connections and buy tickets. She would stop by the auto hire business and arrange to give back her Ford. She would pack and rest. She was glad to be going home.

Chapter 28

That next day was a busy one for some other people too. Now that it was mid-April, Moraig Dunne's garden was flourishing. She preferred to use young herbs for her medicines, so she was occupied with harvesting the new green growths. Some were hung up to dry in a cool, dark attic.

The whole attic space was redolent with the aromas of basil, sage, dill and rosemary. Hidden among the herbs were clusters of white poppies and clusters of blue lobelias. No one entered that attic but Moraig.

She hoped someday to teach Lily her craft, but so far it didn't seem possible. Lily was flighty, unfocused and she could not read, write or speak. And it was Moraig's fault.

When Moraig learned that her daughter, Trilby, was pregnant, she fed the girl lobelia. She couldn't use a willow stick on her own daughter.

Lobelia made Trilby ill with abdominal cramps and diarrhea. It did not end the pregnancy. But Moraig feared it had damaged the fetus. It did damage Trilby's internal organs, her liver, kidneys and colon. Ultimately, lobelia caused Trilby's death.

Moraig felt guilty about her daughter, but she also thought that perhaps Tony Lewis should share the blame. He should have sent the girl home instead of inviting her into his bed.

On a certain evening about a fortnight ago, Moraig was leaving the home of a patient in Maiden's Heath. She had used reiki, massage and incantation to relieve the headache of a woman of the village. She had some success and her patient was grateful. Moraig had a few shillings in her pocket.

Walking home, she walked past the Rook and Crown Pub and paused a moment to look in the window. And there she saw Tony Lewis, enjoying dinner and ale with the red-haired Joanna.

They were completely wrapped up in each other. She suspected that if they weren't already lovers, they soon would be.

Now, at last, Moraig had a way to get back at him. Joanna Whitfield would pay for his sin and Tony would be devastated at losing her.

Moraig still had those three hairs from Joanna, safely tucked away in her book of Olde Magik. She would use one hair one evening in a spell to gain some control over the woman. Yes. A good way to begin.

Maven Scarlett was uneasy. She sensed that there was unrest in one of her coven sisters. She suspected that something was amiss with Moraig Dunne, but what?

Moraig kept to herself, out in that cottage in the woods. She tried to be observant in her coven's practice, but Maven Scarlett could tell that at times

Moraig was seething. Maven also suspected that, on occasion, Moraig lied.

She'd heard Moraig talk about the old priest's predictions. Maven knew about his foretelling of a young, red-haired magic woman, moving into his house, but she sensed no evil associated with the woman. Maven knew that Moraig had a particular dislike for this lady.

Mother Maven was alarmed when Moraig confessed she had three hairs from the girl's head. She wondered why. Mother knew that years ago, before her last incarnation, some witches used those hairs to cast spells. And most of the spells were harmful. She didn't trust Moraig.

Maven Scarlett was generally satisfied with her life. She and her sisters had given care to the heath and it was healthy again. The coven had been able to celebrate the Spring Equinox on the heath and they were looking forward to celebrating Beltane there. She even had permitted the Christian Brothers to have their Easter Sunrise service there, on their promise that no harm would come to the heath.

But she was tired. She was in her third incarnation, and this one had lasted a very long time. She wasn't sure of her age this cycle. She had stopped counting after her ninetieth birthday.

It was becoming more difficult to maintain her beautiful shell. In this shell she was a crone, ninety-some years old. She wanted to rest, but to do so she must install a replacement. She prayed to the Goddess daily to send someone who would take over for her. So far, there was no one.

Later that same evening Horace McEldoo swore he saw a flash of light coming from Joanna's kitchen window.

He called Hettie to come help him watch, in case that happened again. Of course, she protested, reminding him that Joanna wasn't coming until the next day.

But Horace stood his ground. He said, "Come here, Mrs. McEldoo, if you please. Just watch the kitchen window. You'll see."

So, Hettie and Horace half hid themselves behind their kitchen curtains and watched Joanna's window intently.

"Oh!" Hettie exclaimed.

"What?" Horace demanded.

"Uh, I thought I saw a flash of red hair," Hettie admitted. "But that can't be."

"No, it can't. Unless - - - "

They faced each other, their expression revealing a shared awareness.

"I don't recall her name," Hettie said.

"Nope. Me either," he agreed.

"This is for Joanna's safety," she acknowledged. "I'm happy for that."

"I hope she's the one you saw in the cards," he mused.

"And in my dream. And in my crystals."

Chapter 29

It was early evening when Joanna arrived home. She felt wonderful as she stepped in through her front door. The house always had a safe feeling for her. Frequently she walked from room to room, just sensing the security there. She would do the same now.

Setting her luggage by the stairway she walked slowly through her parlor, looking at every corner and open space. She lit a small lamp and proceeded to open the drapes on each window. She sensed a warmth in the house, warmer than any previous experience.

She entered the next room which served as a dining room, library and office. Though this room was multipurpose, there was no sense of confusion. It was calm and inviting. She turned on the desk lamp and moved onto the kitchen.

Joanna loved her kitchen though she was an inexperienced cook. She planned to ask Hettie McEldoo for lessons and recipes. Happily, she turned on the ceiling light which made her feel safe all over.

She guessed that the McEldoos were watching her home. If so, they saw the lights were on and they would no doubt arrive at her kitchen door soon,

She was correct. In less than three minutes there was an excited rapping on the kitchen door. Hettie and Horace came bursting into the room, arms open to hug Joanna.

"I missed you both so much!" Jo declared. "Is my oak tree alright?"

Horace smiled and assured her that the tree was thriving. "We kept watch over it and your house," he said. "And you found your Aunt Elspeth. How wonderful," Hettie said happily and realized that Elspeth was the name she tried to recall earlier.

"I did, and she exceeded all my expectations. She's amazing," Joanna sighed. "I learned so much about my family. I come from a line of powerful women. They were healers, protectors and many could predict events. There were midwives too, and herbalists." Here Joanna stopped to catch her breath.

There was silence for a moment, Joanna remembering her visit with her aunt while the McEldoos wondered how much she understood.

Casually, Hettie got up, filled Joanna's kettle and put it on to heat. Jo apologized instantly, saying, "I'm so sorry. I should have offered you a 'cuppa'." Horace reached across the table and patted Jo's hand. "Nay, child, don't bother yourself. You've had a busy day."

"Yes, I have," she agreed. Then, "Did you know that Tony Lewis rang me up at the bed and breakfast?"

"No, I did not! And I did not give him the phone number. You said not to," declared a very indignant

Hettie. Horace shook his head. "But you did say the Blue Moon B&B in Fort William."

"I never!" she insisted.

"'Fraid you did, Hettie," Horace said. "I heard you."

"God forgive me," Hettie pleaded. "I never meant it."

Joanna was not upset and she told her friends so. "It's alright," she insisted. "He only called once. He wanted to come home tomorrow, but I asked him to wait a few days longer."

She thought for a minute before saying, "I need a few days to sort my thoughts about him. And I need to talk to him about Lily - - - and Moraig."

Horace took Joanna's hand and squeezed it gently. "Avoid Moraig. I suspect that Lily is harmless, but Moraig can't be trusted. She may be a danger to both you and Mr. Lewis. But don't worry. The missus and I are always ready to help."

Hettie added, "And no doubt Elspeth will be here too, right?"

"It's difficult to answer that. She said she'd never be far away, but sometimes she might be in a different form. She said I'd always recognize her."

Information like this was new to Joanna, but she believed everything Elspeth said. She could tell that the McEldoos believed, too.

Hettie squeezed Joanna's other hand and confessed, "Darlin' she's been here already. I saw her red hair last night as she flashed by a window."

"Wonderful. And you know what? I am no longer afraid of Moraig. Now that I know the power that courses through my bloodline, I can protect myself against anything."

"But I am so grateful for you two," Joanna admitted and she squeezed their hands in return. As she said the words a weariness overtook her. She said, "I didn't realize how tired I am." She yawned shamelessly

The McEldoos, as one, rose to their feet and apologized profusely for keeping her from her bed. They let themselves out .and Joanna, suitcase in hand, climbed the stairs to her room. She changed into a nighty and crawled into bed. Sleep came instantly.

Chapter 30

Joanna slept deeply that night. She wakened next morning feeling happy to be in her own room and bed. She would have stayed in bed longer, but her clock marked the time as ten a.m. To her surprise she didn't recall any dreams from the night's slumber.

She sat on the side of the bed for a short while, trying to recall events from the day before. She remembered the train rides from Fort William to Glasgow then Glasgow to London. Joanna knew she could have stayed in London for the night, but she felt compelled to go on home.

"No wonder I was so tired," she thought. "A quick shower will help."

And it did help. She went down the stairs, humming a bit on her way to the kitchen. She opened a window to let in the fresh English country air and put the kettle on the heat. She would enjoy having a few cups of tea while she pondered her future.

Moraig was happy this morning. Last evening, she spent time planning her strategy. She had read the cards, studied the sky and stars. She lit black candles and took note of the direction of the flames flickering. She interpreted the findings and they led to one conclusion: do it tonight.

Moraig planned to make Joanna suffer. Not that Joanna had done anything to the old witch. And Moraig wasn't afraid of any power that Joanna might have. No, the girl must suffer so that Tony Lewis would suffer too. Moraig would have the revenge she so wanted.

But where was Tony Lewis? Moraig searched her inner core and senses, trying to ascertain his whereabouts. She felt he was far from home. Odd, because his lovely Joanna was back in Maiden's Heath. *He'll be back soon*, she thought. She wanted him to see his love's anguish. Moraig didn't intend to kill the girl. No, but sometimes her powers were so strong ---.

Tonight, she would take one of the red hairs from their hiding place. She would use her small pallet made of hard ash. Long ago she'd painted a symbol on it, the Egyptian Eye of Horus. Some witches used this symbol to assure protection for themselves, as Moraig had done many times.

Lately though, she'd been using it to increase her clairvoyant powers and she found it to be very effective. This night she would use it to cast a spell on Joanna, where the girl would be obedient to Moraig and do what she was told.

Today, malevolent energy permeated Moraig's cottage as she planned the spell she would perform that evening. The energy inside her home was like an electric surge. Usually dormant, now the air was alive and threatening,

Lily awoke that evening, sensing something was wrong. Lily didn't talk, but she did hear everything. And she did see. She didn't readily understand what she saw, but given some time, she could comprehend well enough.

This evening she was sensing an oppressive atmosphere within the home she shared with Moraig. Lily got out of bed and walked silently to her grandmother's room. There she watched at the doorway as her grandmother took down the large, heavy book from the shelf.

Lily couldn't read the title of the book, but she'd seen Moraig look through it often. This time, Lily saw Moraig open the book and take a golden thread from it.

The girl watched from a shadowy place as her grandmother went to the communing room and sat on the floor by an altar. Moraig held the hair between her two hands as though keeping it warm.

Moraig held the thread thus for a long time, while her lips moved, mumbling, chanting. Then she dropped the hair into her copper sacrament vessel. She continued chanting while she set a fire in the pot.

The fire flashed blue, then white; then it sizzled, then it was gone. No smoke was visible, but a sweet odor like forsythia, hung in the air for a long time.

It was as though Moraig drew strength from the

fire. She sat up straighter, her mumbling louder and clearer. Lily could discern many of the chanted words: "red hair, girl, punish him." She couldn't understand revenge. She didn't know a 'him.' But 'red hair' and 'girl' struck a familiar chord in her memory, though it was a dim, vague memory.

It was more than Lily was capable of, to come to a conclusion about Moraig, the red hairs and whoever 'him' was. However, she could sense the disruption in the energy of the house. She was afraid.

Lily was weary and was wanting her bed when Moraig stood up. Lily scurried to her bed and pulled her covers up to her chin before Moraig peeked into her bedroom.

Lily knew she should feign sleep. Moraig watched from the doorway for a brief time, then left.

The girl continued to lie very still for as long as she could. She could hear Moraig moving about in the communing room. Then she heard the house door open and close.

Wondering if her grandmother had left, Lily stole into the communing room. Finding it empty, she went to a front window and peered out. She could barely see it, but it was there: a torch moving down the path, away from the house.

She wondered where her grandmother was going.

Chapter 31

It was the deepest part of the night when Moraig returned to her cottage. She immediately went to check on Lily, who was fast asleep. Finally, the old witch sat on her bed and with closed eyes, mentally retraced her steps of the evening.

She'd used her torch to guide her safely though her woods, but when she reached the road, she turned it off. The moonlight would be enough, she reasoned. She had about four miles to walk, though without having to drag Lily along behind her, she could run and make good time. *An hour to get there, thirty minutes to scout around the area, then another hour to get home.* It could be done.

In about half an hour, she reached Maiden's Heath. She scurried along the High Street, being careful to stay in the shadows. When she reached the far end of the town, she knew she had only one mile to go.

Moraig clipped along at a respectable pace, without a hint of fatigue. Her determination had remained constant. Her goal this night, to find entry to the house. Then she would find the path from the house, through the woods, to the heath. Getting back home would be easy.

When she was passing the McEldoo home, she'd

sensed unrest in the house. It had caused her to stop and listen for a few seconds. She was certain the couple hadn't heard her footsteps. However, the McEldoo woman was known to be a sensitive. Still, Moraig went on to the next house, Joanna Whitfield's home.

Moraig stole up to the house and flattened herself against it. Slowly, she crept along the east wall of the exterior, feeling for a low window. Near the back of the house, she found what she needed.

The window had been neglected for many months, at least. It was covered with spider webs, dirt and mud. Moraig suspected the window must be behind something. She found she was correct for though she cleared the window as best she could, she still hadn't been able to see inside.

Luckily, the window wasn't stuck. It slid up with just a little encouragement. Moraig reached in and her hands touched the back of a wooden cabinet.

With a firm push from Moraig, the cabinet moved a couple inches away. It was on wheels! Surely, Moraig's plans were working.

She was able to pull the cabinet back, closer to the window, so no one inside could tell it had been moved. Before she closed the window completely, she found some tiny stones on the ground and scattered six or seven of them inside the window sill. She closed the window to within one-half inch of its bottom, thanks to the stones. It would open easily the next time she tried.

She made her way home without delay.

Moraig laid down, still fully dressed. She was asleep instantly, too tired to dream.

<h1 style="text-align:center">Chapter 32</h1>

The next morning Joanna had difficulty waking up. She felt like she was caught in a powerful dream, almost awake, but not finished dreaming. It took great determination to come to a sitting position, her legs dangling over the side. Still blaming her recent spree in Scotland for her fatigue, she reasoned that soon she would be back to her normal self.

She thought that if she wrote a journal about her trip, it would help her focus better and lift the fog from her mind. Joanna would begin her journal with her train ride to Glasgow. She wrote a few sentences and was satisfied with them. Her grammar wasn't perfect, nor was her spelling. It was the message she wanted to record. For her eyes only.

After about ten minutes of writing Joanna was feeling weary. Her eyelids were feeling heavy. She closed her journal, then closed her eyes. Sleep came immediately.

She was wakened by someone knocking smartly on her door. She was still a bit dazed when she went to see who was making all that noise.

The postman was waiting there with a package wrapped in brown paper. "Miss Whitfield?" he asked.

He pushed a clipboard toward her, quickly followed by a greasy writing pen. "Sign your name by the X," he instructed.

"I'll get my own pen." Joanna insisted, and abruptly ran into the house. She returned seconds later with her own pen and scrawled her signature on the page.

"Here," the postman insisted, and shoved the parcel into her arms. He sprinted to his van and sped away.

Joanna was pretty sure she knew what the package contained, and when she saw the Scotland postmark, she was absolutely certain. She tore the paper open and was delighted to see her kilt.

She held the garment up to her body, then spread the kilt on the dining room table to inspect it. It was exquisite.   The woven pattern was perfect, the MacDonald of the Isles Ancient Hunting tartan, with soft hues of blue and green. She would wear it at the first opportunity.

A feeling of profound fatigue overtook her. Deciding she was probably hungry; she made her way to the kitchen and poured a glass of tomato juice from the refrigerator. After adding a quick shake of salt to it, she drank it right down.

After a minute or two she felt a bit stronger. She made some toast, applied a thin coat of butter and heaps of bitter, orange marmalade. It was delicious.

After two cups of strong tea, Jo felt more awake, but still tired. She didn't know what, if anything, she'd be able to do today.

Joanna walked slowly around her kitchen, then into the dining room, where she lightly touched chair backs and table tops as she passed them. The furniture was all her own, she knew that. Yet, why didn't they collapse when she touched them? They were supposed to; she was sure of that.

For some reason, she needed to be outdoors. Leaving by the kitchen door, she came to the circle where the oak tree stood. She was satisfied to see that the tree had grown and was fuller. She studied it for a moment, wondering if the tree would rise up from the ground and fly away. She recognized this as a crazy thought, but still expected it to happen.

Joanna saw that she had a companion on her walk. A large, sleek, ginger-coated cat was just beside her feet. The cat looked at Jo as if waiting for her to make a move.

Jo didn't know when the cat had joined her. She seemed to have materialized out of nowhere. As Jo walked a few steps away from her house, the cat walked with her. Jo noticed the cat had beautiful, bright green eyes.

Soon they reached the heath. Its peacefulness pleased her, but she had no idea why she was there. Still she walked a few steps further in.

Joanna sat on the ground, oblivious to the dampness. The sun had not yet burned off the dew, but it was still morning and Jo didn't mind the wet grass. The cat curled up next to her.

Jo had always thought of the heath as a dichotomy, possessing memories of both goodness and evil, of burning and being restored. If she sat completely still, she could hear the cries of the young ladies who hadn't passed the maiden's test. She could hear the jubilant laughter of those who did pass.

Sleep overtook her. She lay down and in a tick of a moment was asleep. The ginger cat left.

Chapter 33

Hettie and Horace McEldoo were having a leisurely breakfast. Every morning they ate the same meal, porridge, eggs, toast and tea. Horace was a slight man, but his appetite was big: three eggs and a huge bowl of porridge, with butter, cream and sugar.

His wife marveled at his intake and lack of fat. Horace always reminded her that he was a hardworking farmer. He burned off as many calories as he ate. She didn't tell him about the times she'd caught him napping under a tree.

On this particular morning, Horace took his second cup of tea with him and stood at the open back door. He let his gaze take in everything, but nothing in particular until he saw an orange cat coming out of the back woods.

He called his wife to him. "Hettie! Come here and bring your driving glasses!"

She'd been clearing away the breakfast dishes and wasn't happy to be interrupted. "Wait 'alf a mo," she stated in native dialect.

"Nay! Now!" Horace insisted.

So, she lay down her dishcloth and walked to the

door, driving glasses perched on her nose.

"Look out there, coming out of the woods," he directed.

"Well I'll be!" she exclaimed. "I haven't seen that girl around here before."

"How do ya know it's a girl?"

"Just watch her step, how delicate it is," Hettie explained.

The ginger cat was at a trot, running purposefully toward the house. However, she stopped short of the porch and sat on the path, meowing loudly.

"That female isn't a stray, you know." Hettie maintained. Horace agreed saying, "She's telling us something, for sure, but I don't know what. I'm gonna walk outside and see what she does."

He opened the screen door and carefully stepped out on the porch. The cat stayed perfectly still. Horace took another step toward the feline, then another. As he attempted one more step, the cat ran a few feet back toward the woods.

"What's goin' on?" Hettie called from the house.

Horace didn't answer, but waved impatiently at his wife, telling her to be quiet.

Hettie was not willing to wait silently. She saw how her husband was stepping cautiously toward the cat and she saw the cat retreat. Hettie tiptoed toward Horace

It seemed the feline was leading them to the woods and she wanted to know why, and can a cat really do that? She'd never heard of such a thing.

They followed the ginger animal into the woods. The cat obviously had an advantage: she could scamper over fallen branches and twigs. She easily leapt over stumps of long forgotten trees and often waited unperturbed while the McEldoos picked their way past the natural impediments.

When they reached the edge of the heath, the cat ran on ahead.

The McEldoos quickened their pace, but the cat disappeared from sight. However, Hettie saw something else ahead. She shouted, "Look over there, Horace."

About one hundred feet away lay the body of a woman. "She's a redhead," Hettie whispered, as though the figure could hear her. "That could be Joanna!"

They reached her quickly. Hettie pronounced that it was indeed Joanna. She bent down and lightly touched the tousled red hair.

Horace asked gently, "Is she alive?"

Hettie didn't answer immediately. Instead, she touched the girl's face. "She's warm," she shared. Hettie rubbed the girl's arm and shoulder, calling her name again.

There was no response.

"Give her a good shake," Horace insisted. When Hettie stared at him in disbelief, Horace bent down, took hold of the girl's shoulders and shook her energetically.

Joanna opened her eyes and fought back. In her confusion she cried out for help. Hettie pushed Horace away and comforted the bewildered girl. Hettie helped her to a sitting position and quieted her.

"Why did you bring me here?" Joanna demanded, crying through frustration.

Horace bent down close to her, saying, "Nay, lass. We found you here. A ginger cat brought us to you."

Joanna scratched her head in disbelief. "How did I get here?" she asked. "You know, I was dreaming I was with Aunt Elspeth."

"Tell us what you remember," Horace said.

Though in a foggy state of mind Joanna slowly gathered her thoughts and arranged them in some logical order.

"You take your time," Hettie assured her.

"I've no other choice," Jo remarked. "My thoughts are a complete puzzle." A pause, then, "I need to stand up."

With Hettie on her right arm and Horace on her left, Jo was half lifted to her feet. She was a bit lightheaded, but she stood.

Finally, she said, "The last thing I remember, I'd just finished breakfast. Toast, I think. But I was so tired. Sleepy, too, I don't' remember how I got to the heath."

Started by a thought, she blurted out, "Was Aunt Elspeth with me? She said she'd always be around." Horace said nothing, but Hettie averred there was no limit to Elspeth's powers.

The three began their walk back through the woods without the red cat making her presence known. They reached Joanna's house without incident.

Horace led Joanna to her parlor and made her comfortable on her sofa while Hettie stayed behind in the kitchen. Joanna guessed that Hettie would fire up the kettle, but before that was done, Hettie ran over to her own house.

Joanna and Horace heard the screen door slam shut. Horace went to the door just in time to see his wife scurrying across the yards. "She must need something from the house," Horace called to Joanna.

Hettie was out of sight for twenty minutes -- he timed her -- when she reappeared, she sort of trotted back to Jo's house. Horace hurried to put the kettle on and get out beakers and tea when his wife came rushing in.

Chapter 34

Hettie entered Joanna's home at a run. She didn't stop until she reached the parlor and plopped into a big, comfy chair. In her hand she clutched a large bunch of green vegetation, roots attached.

"What on earth is that?" Joanna asked, getting herself upright on the sofa.

"This?" Hettie responded, holding up the bunch of long-stemmed green herbs. "This is Angelica. It's to protect you."

At this, Hettie rose to her feet and proceeded to each corner of the parlor, leaving a stem of Angelica there, en garde. Next, she went to the dining room and placed Angelica in each corner. Then on to the kitchen to continue her mission, leaving an Angelica soldier stationed at the same crucial points.

When Hettie started up the stairs to the second floor, Joanna stopped her. "Please wait," she begged. "What are you doing?"

"Let me put these in your bedroom first. Then I'll explain." Huffing and puffing, Hettie conquered the stairs and placed protective Angelica in Joanna's bedroom.

Returning to the parlor, Hettie sat down next to Joanna. She reached over and took the younger woman's hand in her own. When her breathing eased, she told Joanna about Angelica, its properties, its usefulness. Especially its ability to repel a curse.

There was silence for a few minutes. Joanna didn't want to ask the question that was overriding every other thought on her mind. Finally, she turned to face Hettie. She could read the answer on Hettie's face.

"Who is trying to hurt me?" Joanna asked.

Without hesitation Hettie answered, "I suspect Moraig Dunne."

"But why?" Joanna demanded.

Hettie gave Jo's hand a squeeze then began. "Do you recall what I told you about Lily? Her mother Trilby?"

"You said that Tony was Lily's father, Trilby died."

"That's right," Hettie concurred.

"But what does that have to do with me?"

Hettie confessed that she wasn't absolutely certain, but her suspicion of Moraig had merit. "How did you feel yesterday?" she asked the girl.

Joanna had to think for a moment, but the answer came to her. "Well, I was quite busy yesterday. Remember, I was on my way back from Scotland. I rode trains most of the day, then I drove here from London late in the day."

"You slept well last night?" Hettie surmised.

"Yes indeed."

Hettie continued, "How were you this morning?"

"Still sleepy! I couldn't seem to get fully awake." Jo thought about this, then remembered something more. "Someone pounded on my front door. He gave me a package. That's it on the table."

Horace retrieved the package. When Jo opened it she remembered that her kilt had arrived. "That woke me. But not for long."

"What happened next?" Hettie prodded.

I'm not sure," Jo said. "I'm so confused. I went outside. I remember the orange cat. The next thing I knew you were shaking me, Horace. I don't know how I got to the heath."

"There's a powerful force at play here," Horace said solemnly.

All three were quiet, deep in thought, when the phone rang brutishly, violently startling everyone.

"What the Hell!" Horace shouted.

"I'll get it," Joanna declared, hurrying to stop the jangling nuisance. Her next word was, "Tony."

Chapter 35

Hettie McEldoo was delighted to find that Tony was in the Boston airport, waiting for his flight home. Joanna, however, was not. Hettie claimed she couldn't understand Joanna's feelings.

It was difficult for Jo to explain why she didn't want to see Tony yet. With some frustration she demanded, "Didn't you hear what I said on the phone!"

"Not really, dear. You spoke very softly," Hettie replied, a hint of reprimand in her voice.

"I'm sorry. You didn't deserve that," Jo said, trying to make amends. She walked the few steps back to the sofa and curled up in her familiar corner. All were quiet, allowing Joanna time to gather her thoughts. She closed her eyes and searched inwardly for a place to begin.

When she opened her eyes again, the McEldoo couple had moved to the kitchen. They welcomed her as she joined them. Horace filled her a cup of newly made tea; Hettie handed her a cookie.

Joanna began. "The events of this morning have frightened and confused me. I don't understand why Morag Dunne dislikes me. I really don't. I've never insulted her, that I'm aware of. I am uncomfortable in her presence and she senses it."

"The only connection I have with her, that I can see, is Tony. I can see why she'd be angry with him, but why take it out on me?"

Hettie had a response to this. She said, "Moraig must believe that harming you will cause him extreme pain, I think she blames him for Trilby's death. If he hadn't gotten Trilby pregnant, Moraig wouldn't have had to give the girl those toxic herbs. So, if you are harmed -- or killed -- she'll have her revenge."

It took Joanna quite a few minutes to mentally digest all this. Suddenly she began to laugh and cry simultaneously. She was drying her tears and between bouts of laughter was repeating, "This is ridiculous" like a mantra.

Horace decided to speak for Hettie and himself when he said, "Dear. We don't understand."

Joanna said, "I know you don't. There's a lot more I need to tell you."

"You can tell us anything," Horace assured her.

"You know we love you like a daughter," Hettie assured her.

"I know you do. I believe you," Joanna answered. "Well, here goes."

"I thought I was in love with Tony Lewis. I may still be. But when I learned about him being Lily's father, I lost some respect for him. He was the adult and he allowed that girl into his house and into his bed. He took advantage of her."

"But Trilby - - - " Hettie began.

"I remember. You told me that Trilby was wild. But like I said, he was the adult."

"There's more," Joanna said, and the tears and laughter began again.

"Well, it must be funny," Horace surmised.

"No! It's ridiculous!" Jo stated.

Joanna took a long drink from her tea cup, then still chuckling announced, "I think I'm pregnant."

No words were said. Horace and Hettie sat in a stunned silence, while Joanna still laughed and cried.

When she could collect herself, she added, "Tony doesn't know. And I don't want him to know."

Hettie gasped, "Oh my Dear." She went to Joanna and gave her a motherly hug. "We'll help you Dear. You're a daughter to us."

Horace jumped to his feet and raising his tea cup to proclaim, "We'll be grandparents."

At this, Joanna broke into fierce sobbing and admitted, "I don't even know if I want this baby!" And she sobbed even louder after that.

She heard Horace say, "Well, I'll be," and opening her eyes and quieting her sobs, she saw that the ginger cat had joined them. The cat boldly jumped into Joanna's lap and purred loudly.

Joanna looked into the cat's green eyes and asked, "Elspeth?"

Chapter 36

Moraig went to the heath early that day, mainly to see if her curse worked. She got there in time to see the pesky McEldoo couple leading Joanna home. She also spied an orange cat. Moraig had not seen this cat before. She was curious about it. She thought it kept too close to Joanna; it surely wasn't a stray,

Well, she thought, *the curse had worked. But how did the McEldoos know to look for that redhead in the heath?*

There were things happening that Moraig hadn't planned on. She intended to repeat her curse at dusk this evening. She would use more oil in her caldron and the fire would be hotter and last longer.

I'll get her to the heath at dawn and make her walk the line, Moraig thought. *She won't see a thing through the blindfold. I think I'll just leave her there and let her wander off.*

When she got home, Lily wasn't in the garden, which was her favorite spot. Instead, Moraig found Lily fast asleep in her bed.

Just as well, Moraig thought! *She's of no help to me in this plan of mine.*

Later that afternoon, Lily was awake, but staying away from her grandmother. She watched Moraig from the kitchen window as the older woman tended her herb gardens, going from one bed to another, thinning stems, deadheading flowers, pulling weeds.

When Moraig started back toward the cottage, Lily sought safety in her own little room. She waited there quietly until she heard her grandmother go up the attic stairs. Lily knew that the attic would keep Moraig busy for a while, so she had time to think.

Lily knew that the atmosphere in her home had changed. She knew it was Moraig that was making her uneasy, although Lily couldn't have put that into words. She remembered her grandmother's strange behavior the previous evening, and became frightened.

Instinct had directed Lily to stay out of Moraig's way, yet later in the day when the sun was setting, Lily tiptoed silently out of her room. She saw Moraig go into her own room and as Lily watched, Moraig again took down the big, heavy book from the top of her cupboard. Moraig opened the book to a certain page and took something from it.

Lily remembered her grandmother doing the same things last night. And when Moraig sat down facing her altar and caused a fire to flare in her cauldron, Lily sensed the danger in the air.

She would watch Moraig and wait to see if the old woman went out again this night. And when Moraig left the cottage that night, Lily was ready. The girl already had shoes on and a jumper over her dress. She also had in her pocket the third red hair. Lily had no idea why she took the hair, and the old Book of Magik was heavy to take down from the cabinet. But something led her to take this hair.

Lily gave the old woman a bit of a head start, then she set out to follow her. She could see Moraig's torch ahead and she didn't want to follow too closely. Instinctively, she slowed her pace. She couldn't predict what Moraig would do if her presence was discovered. There were times in the past when Lily's grandmother had taken a switch to the girl's backside. Moraig would say, "You're a bad girl! Bad!" Lily would cry. The switch hurt. She never wanted to be bad again. But she had to follow Moraig. She didn't know why. She only sensed that her home was different and so was Moraig.

Chapter 37

Joanna finally convinced the McEldoos to go home that night. She locked all the doors and windows -- well, all but one window. Perhaps she didn't know about that window in the kitchen, behind the china cabinet. Or maybe she simply forgot. But somehow that window didn't get locked.

Joanna was certain that the orange cat, if not Aunt Elspeth transformed, was at least a guardian and a protector. When she convinced the McEldoos of this, they agreed to go home.

Hettie made Joanna promise to ring them if she heard anything suspicious. And Joanna pointed out that Hettie had placed enough Angelica throughout the house to ward off any curse.

So, Hettie and Horace went home, albeit reluctantly.

"I'm really worried about her," Hettie confided to her husband.

"I'm sure y'are," Horace answered. "I don't know what else to do."

"I'll keep vigil from our kitchen window," Hettie declared.

"Let me get a bit o' sleep and then I'll' take over,"

Horace offered. He added, "I told our girl if she's scared by somethin', just turn on her bedroom lamp. We'll be right over."

Moraig set out on her night-time trek intending to actually enter the house this time. She would get in through the kitchen window, then unlock the kitchen door for an easy escape.

She didn't know what she might encounter. Possibly one or both McEldoos would be staying with Joanna. They were like that. Do-gooders.

Then too, that orange cat might be around. Moraig was certain this was no ordinary cat. But if she thought realistically about it, orange cats didn't have powers; no, not like black cats did. Of course, Maven Scarlett's silver cat, Goddess Aoefe, was the most powerful feline in existence.

Moraig knew she was being followed by Lily. She didn't have to look behind her to sense Lily's presence. Moraig chuckled and thought *Lily's curious. Good. Maybe she'll turn out to be a helper after all.*

Soon Moraig came to the village, Maiden's Heath. As before, she slunk along in the shadows next to the buildings. Lily followed her still, but by the time Moraig came to the end of the High Street, she realized Lily was no longer there. *I suspect she's gone home,* Moraig thought. The old woman continued on her way. She was determined to succeed.

Chapter 38

Lily was able to trail her grandmother easily. There was no one else out and about. There were no dogs or cats around to distract her. When she came to the alley that led to the mews, she recognized it and knew she had to go in that direction. She was able to pull her thoughts together enough to know that this was the way to the 'Woman Who Knows' the woman Moraig called 'Mother".

The young girl had no thoughts or words to explain her feelings. She only knew that she must get to Mother Maven. Some magic force was pulling her in the direction she must go.

When she saw the light above the purple door, she ran to it. A quick RAP on the door brought the esteemed lady. Maven Scarlett, seeing Lily alone at the door, smiled kindly and said, "So the time has come."

In response, Lily took the third red hair from her pocket and handed it to Mother Maven.

It didn't take them long to get there. Maven Scarlett simply took Lily by the hand, told her to close her eyes and hold tight. Lily felt her hair being blown by the wind, just for a bit then her feet touched the cool earth. She opened her eyes and found that she and Mother were standing amid a copse of trees, out of sight from the old woman who was trying to enter the house through a window.

Moraig found the window unlocked, but still barricaded by the wooden cabinet. She immediately sensed the Angelica. *So what*, she thought. *That herb might stop a lesser witch's curse, but not mine.*

She pushed the cabinet easily, remembering that it seemed to be on wheels. She eased herself through the window and immediately unlocked the kitchen door.

The night was dark, the moon only a sliver. Moraig didn't want to chance tripping on something or falling. No, silence was necessary. So, she took a penlight from her pocket and proceeded through the house to find the stairway.

Maven Scarlett saw the glow from the penlight and hurried to the house, pulling Lily along beside her. They entered through the front door of the house. Maven simply touched it and it sprang open.

Maven and Lily climbed the stairs, but stood still at the top to watch Moraig struggling with the orange cat.

Moraig was trying to enter Joanna's bedroom and the orange cat had jumped to her shoulder, hissing and growling and scratching the old woman.

Joanna heard her cat fighting and turned on the lamp. The Angelica had worked; she wasn't in a stupor, like the night before. Horace and Hettie saw the light and rushed to help Joanna.

Maven Scarlett brought it all to a halt. She simply

said, "Stop."   The cat looked at her in stunned reverence and readily jumped down. Moraig, however, began trembling. Perhaps she was angry, or maybe she was frightened. At any rate, she turned slowly, and boldly faced Maven stating, "This is not your concern." Moraig's face became red, and defiantly she said "You can't hurt me. I'm as strong as you are."

She was wrong.

"But you're not as strong as two of us." There stood Elspeth, with her radiant ginger hair and her brilliant green eyes. Her stare frightened Moraig. Mother Maven acknowledged Elspeth's presence, then addressed Moraig: "I didn't come here alone. Lily is here too. Think of her before you do anything."

Maven continued, "You must go away forever, Moraig. Go North. Far North, in Scotland. There's a coven there. A small one. They'll welcome you with your knowledge of herbs and healing. Follow your instincts and you'll find them."

Moraig knew she had no other choice, but quickly asserted, "I'll take Lily with me." Maven hushed her. "No, you won't. I'll keep her with me and restore her senses."

There happened a commotion at the front door and Horace and Hettie came bursting into the house. They rushed up the stairs, but stopped when they saw Maven. They climbed the last three steps slowly. They saw Elspeth and were relieved, for they also saw Moraig.

"Where's Joanna?" Hettie pleaded.

Elspeth reached over and opened the door to Joanna's room. Joanna came to the door and trembled when she saw Moraig. Elspeth calmed her with a kiss on her forehead.

Hettie clasped her own hands together near her heart and lowered her head for a moment, all in respect for Maven Scarlett. Maven, in turn, gently touched Hettie's shoulder saying, "Sweet Sister." She added, "Hettie take Joanna home with you. Now, please."

Joanna left promptly, braced by Horace and Hettie who were tearful and tender. When they reached the McEldoo house, Horace went in first and turned on all the lights. The couple took Joanna into their parlor, where she curled up in a great, overstuffed chair. She asked, "Hettie, who was that woman with the silver hair?"

"My dear, that was Maven Scarlett, leader of the local coven and possibly the most powerful witch ever. They say she has lived more than one lifetime."

"She called you Sister."

"Yes, but she meant I'm a sister to the coven."

"I don't understand," Joanna confessed. "Are you a witch?"

Chapter 39

Hettie chuckled, answering, "No Dear, I'm no witch. I do have some powers, but they are minimal. I'm told I have a tender heart and that is powerful energy."

Jo replied, "I love you both, you know."

"And we love you, Darlin."

Horace handed Joanna a shot glass filled to the brim with brandy. "Here Jo, drink this down," he said.

She did and minutes later she fell asleep, still in her big chair.

Meanwhile, Maven and Elspeth sent Moraig on her way North. Elspeth reminded Moraig that she spent lots of time in Scotland. She would check on Moraig from time to time. Elspeth followed Moraig that night, or rather, the orange cat did. Maven purged the house, smudging every corner and purifying the air.

After that she held Lily's hand and took the girl home.

At some point during the night, Joanna woke up enough to move to the sofa. She wakened in the morning to a beautiful day, feeling hopeful and relaxed. She remembered the danger of the last two days and night, but this morning she somehow knew that the danger was over.

Hettie entered the parlor, flustered and excited. "Joanna! Quick! Run upstairs and take a shower, I'll get to your house and retrieve some clothes. Get going!" Hettie dashed out the door, ignoring the startled expression on the girl's face.

Joanna showered, put on the clean clothes and demanded that Hettie tell her what was going on.

"First let's get a cuppa'," Hettie said, and the two women went to the kitchen. They sat at the table with toast and tea provided by Horace.

"Well!" Jo insisted.

Horace said it bluntly. "You're gettin' company."

"What? Who's coming?" Jo asked.

Right to the point, Horace said, "Tony."

"No!" Joanna insisted.

"Yep," Horace assured her, adding, "any minute now."

"How does he know I'm here?" Joanna demanded angrily.

Hettie admitted telling him. "He rang here an hour ago. Said he rang you first, but got no answer. So, he tries us." A brief pause, then, "I just couldn't lie to him."

All Joanna could say was, "Okay," knowing it would happen sooner or later. Soon Horace and Hettie excused themselves to the parlor and Tony came walking in through the kitchen door.

He sat in the chair across the table from Joanna. He said nothing, but his eyes were questioning her.

Finally, he spoke, "You've changed your mind about me, haven't you?"

She looked away for a second, but then admitted, "No, not changed my mind. Truly I'm confused. I don't' know what to think."

"Think about what?"

Joanna's breathing caught for a moment, but she answered him honestly, "About you and Trilby and Lily."

"Oh." Then, "I hoped you wouldn't find out."

"Don't you think I deserve to know?"

"It has nothing to do with us," he pleaded, becoming noticeably uncomfortable.

"On the contrary! My life was in danger because you got Trilby pregnant and she died!"

"So that's it," he surmised. "Moraig would have killed you to get back at me."

They shared a soft intimate look. Tony reached across the table and took her hands in his. He asked, "What must I do, Joanna. I love you. I want to marry you."

She chuckled and said, "that is a very good thing. There's a lot you don't know about my family. Nothing bad, just - - - unusual."

"Witches?" he asked.

"Good, kind, healing women."

"And you?"

"Possibly," Jo admitted. "There's one more thing I should tell you."

"Oh?"

About the Author

Joanne is a retired RN who lives in the quaint historic town of Ligonier, PA.   After spending a few years composing poetry and vignettes, in 2011 she began writing novels.

She has published a mystery/romance trilogy based in Ireland and featuring Chief Inspector Desmond Joyce of the Garda Siochanna:
The Bed and Breakfast Murder
" ---and Peace Attend Thee"
Three Sisters and a Red Rabbit

This is her newest – *Three Red Hairs*.

All can be purchased through her email jmc.athlone@hotmail.com

She loves to sing, cook, and travels to the U.K. for inspiration.